IU699146

LAST JUDGEMENT

By Anna Clarke

LAST JUDGEMENT

ANNA CLARKE

PUBLISHED FOR THE CRIME CLUB BY
DOUBLEDAY & COMPANY, INC.
GARDEN CITY, NEW YORK
1985

All of the characters in this book
are fictitious, and any resemblance
to actual persons, living or dead,
is purely coincidental.

Library of Congress Cataloging in Publication Data

Clarke, Anna, 1919–
Last judgement.
I. Title.
PR6053.L3248L28   1985   823'.914
ISBN 0-385-19666-0
Library of Congress Catalog Card Number 84-13598

LAST JUDGEMENT

CHAPTER 1

"It would be so easy for Grandpa to die," said James Goff. "He's nearly ninety, and he's got all those things wrong with him—heart disease, asthma, arthritis—"

"You don't *die* of arthritis," said the girl who was sitting opposite him at the big deal table in the kitchen. "It's crippling, but not fatal."

She was a dark-eyed, serious-faced girl about a year older than him, and she was eating spaghetti with an air of great concentration.

"Why do you always have to be so literal, Mary? You know perfectly well what I mean."

Mary Morrison did not reply until she had removed the dirty plates and put some cheese and a bowl of fruit on the table. Then she said very quietly and without looking at her companion, "I know exactly what you mean, and I wish you wouldn't talk like that."

"Why?" James helped himself to an apple, noticed that it had a bruise mark on it, made a grimace, replaced it in the bowl and took another. Mary watched him without comment but with the faintest of smiles on her face, half-ironic, half-indulgent.

"Why does it upset you to talk about his death?" James continued. "After all, he can't last much longer, and with all his ailments he can't have much joy in life. You're not going to pretend that you truly care for your stepfather, I hope. That's the last thing you are—a hypocrite. In fact, I think you are the most honest person I've ever known."

Mary flushed and frowned at her apple—the imperfect one that James had put aside. She was shy and compliments embarrassed her, particularly when they came from James.

"It's because I know you're sincere that I find it so difficult to understand," he went on. "Grandpa simply takes it for granted that you give up your entire life to looking after this house and running about for him every moment of the day and night and putting up with all his moods and—"

"I don't look after him at night," interrupted Mary. "Hector Greenaway gets him to bed and gets him up."

"Revolting little man. I don't trust him an inch. There's something about a male nurse—"

"That isn't on a par with a university lecturer?"

James laughed. "I like it when you're bitchy, Mary. It shows that you've still got an ego of your own, even after all these years of ministering to every whim of our greatest living novelist."

"It's only five years since Mother died," Mary pointed out.

"And she'd had more than twenty years of it. How she put up with him for all that time I don't know. My granny only stuck it for half as long before she ran away."

"Your grandmother had wealthy parents and a comfortable home to run away to. My mother had an illegitimate baby and no money at all."

Mary spoke with great emotion. When she felt strongly about anything she could forget her shyness, and her rather brooding face acquired a strange beauty. "He gave her a home and a name and a position in life. She liked being Mrs. G. E. Goff, even though he bullied her and sneered at her ignorance. She enjoyed the reflected glory. I know he's a vindictive and tyrannical old man, but—but —" Mary bit her lip. She was suddenly near to tears. "I don't remember any other home except this house, and he's the only father I've ever known."

"I see," said James.

"You don't see at all!" cried Mary. "You don't know anything about poverty and dependence and insecurity. Oh yes, I know you lost your parents when you were only two years old, but you did know exactly who they were and who you were, and you were brought up in great comfort by an adoring grandmother who still adores you, and everyone was sorry for you and wanted to make it up to you, and you were clever and good-looking and had the education you wanted and the career you wanted, and the only thing lacking was that your famous grandfather didn't want to know you because of the family feud, and now that's been put right too. That's his bell. I expect he's finished his supper."

"I wish he'd wait until we've finished ours," said James, but she had already left the room and did not hear him.

He got up from the table, moved some knives and plates about in a desultory way as if he was thinking of washing up; changed his mind and ran water into the kettle but decided after all to leave it to Mary to make the coffee; moved around the kitchen and stared at the old-fashioned dresser and the cupboards and the sink and the red-and-yellow window curtains that shut out the November night, as if the room contained some secret that would yield itself to him if only he concentrated on it long enough; and finally came out into the hall and stood at the foot of the staircase.

It was a large, rambling and inconvenient house, built at a time when land was cheap in this part of South London and domestic servants were plentiful. But there were no cooks and gardeners and housemaids here now; only a woman who helped with the cleaning two mornings a week, the male nurse who looked after the old man at night, and Mary herself. Yet the house always looked clean and tidy and the garden well cared for. James took time off from the consideration of his own hopes and ambitions in order to wonder how on earth Mary managed it. His own grandmother, G. E. Goff's first wife, could not have done it, and nor could any of the other women whom James had known, and he had a large and varied acquaintance.

Mary Morrison really was the most extraordinary girl. She was full of old-fashioned virtues like patience and loyalty and duty, the sort of qualities that could be particularly valuable to those who did not themselves possess them; the sort of qualities that might even tempt one into thinking of getting married.

James's mind shied away from the thought. Up till now he had successfully avoided any personal commitment. But then he had never before met anybody quite like Mary. It was her very virtues that made it so difficult—it would have been much easier if she had been more selfish, less scrupulous, perhaps even less intelligent. With a different sort of girl one could speak straight out. One could say something like,

"He's enormously famous and very rich. He's very old and he can't last long. Who is going to get what he leaves? Not just the money, but the rest of the legacy, the famous Goff Papers, all those manuscripts and diaries and letters and God knows what other documents stashed away in that study of his upstairs that most of the libraries and learned institutions in Britain and America would give anything to get hold of. You write all his letters, Mary, and make all his phone calls. You must know if he has made a will. Are you named yourself? Am I? After all, I'm the nearest blood relation, the direct descendant, the next of kin, and he seems to have forgiven my grandma for de-

serting him, and he seems to like me, but nevertheless
. . ."

Every time he came to Number 12 Chestnut Close,
James Goff had just such a speech in his mind, but the
moment he saw Mary Morrison he knew it would be impossible to make it. Different tactics were needed, but so
far, although he had been seeing her at least twice a week
for the past six months, he had not yet persuaded her to
tell him. All he could do was drop a hint to her now and
then and make himself as charming to her as possible. So
far the hints had only served to confirm the strength of
what he was up against, which left him with no weapon
but one, and that one seemed to be turning into a two-
edged sword.

Or a boomerang. It was by no means the first time that
James Goff had set out to make a woman fall in love with
him, but on all those other occasions he had known that
the affair was not going to last for very long.

It was not so with Mary.

James Goff stared at his reflection in the big mirror that
hung over the telephone table in the hall and said to
himself that it was going to end with him marrying her
because that was the only way to make sure of the Goff
Papers.

He made a face into the mirror and then laughed at
himself. *Aspern Papers* stuff. It was quite absurd. But then
life did so often copy literature. As a teacher of English
and a writer and critic of some reputation he knew that
very well. And, after all, the thought of marrying Mary
Morrison was not *so* dreadful. On the contrary. She was a
very different sort of creature from the dim heroine of the
Henry James story. There were unknown depths in Mary
and it would be interesting to explore them. There was
fascination, too, in the fact that so little was known about
her natural father, except that he could not have pos-

sessed the sort of loyalty and integrity that was such an
outstanding characteristic in Mary herself.

Was this integrity so unassailable? James found himself
hoping that it was not. For even with Mary on his side,
there would probably be situations in which some sort of
—well, call it preventative measures—might become necessary before he could get possession of the Goff Papers. If
there was a risk that the old man might bequeath them to
somebody else, for instance, then James would be prepared to take some drastic action. But would Mary? How
far would she go for his sake?

James made another grimace and then turned away
from the mirror, half-ashamed of the direction that his
thoughts were taking and half-frightened by it. Love and
ambition. Each one alone was a very powerful force—
numerous examples in both life and literature could bear
witness to that. And if you combined these two forces . . .
James tried to think of an outstanding literary example,
but failed. It seemed to be very difficult to concentrate his
thoughts this evening.

But I am not a villainous sort of person, he thought as he
moved into the front sitting-room, which was over-fur-
nished with chintz-covered armchairs and tiresome little
tables and tasteless ornaments; I am no worse than anybody else. It's perfectly natural that I should want G. E.
Goff's papers so that I can write the first authentic biography. After all, I am his natural heir. If it hadn't been for
the family feud, there'd have been no question about my
having them, and all his money too. And that feud was not
my fault; I was not even born then.

He moved over to the great bay window, near to which
stood the little walnut bureau where Mary kept her own
personal papers and where she sat to write letters. The
flap was down, and on the blotter lay a cheque-book and a
little pile of household accounts. Everything looked very

tidy. James longed to open some of the drawers, but dared not. Mary might come in at any moment. The whole house, hall and staircase and all, was thickly carpeted. It was almost uncanny how little one heard from room to room.

On top of the bureau there stood two photographs. One was of G. E. Goff, the well-known portrait taken on his eightieth birthday, which was reproduced on the jackets of the "Collected Works" published on that occasion, and used for reviews and newspaper articles and all publicity purposes.

It was a striking face, worthy of its owner's unchallenged status as the writer of the century. Long and lean under the thick white hair. No sign of flabbiness, not the least hint of senility in those wide-open eyes and that firm, faintly smiling mouth. But he has changed a lot since then, thought James: They had better not take any pictures of him as he is today, but stick to this portrait for the ninetieth birthday celebration.

He stared for some while at the photograph, oddly stirred by the knowledge that this old man, more like a national monument than like a living human being, was in fact the reason for his own existence; but not recognizing, as blood relations so seldom do, the strong family likeness to the face that he had been looking at a moment or two previously in the hall mirror.

Then he turned to the other photograph. It was an enlarged snapshot, not a studio portrait. It showed a dark-haired, grave-eyed young woman, dressed in the fashions of a quarter of a century ago, sitting on what looked like a bench in a park and holding out her hands to a small child of whom only the back view was visible. The child was dressed in some sort of playsuit and its dark hair was close-cropped. It was difficult to tell whether it was a girl or a boy, but James knew that this was a picture of Mary and her mother, the only one she possessed of the time before G. E. Goff had come into their lives.

It was impossible for G. E. Goff's grandson to look at this photograph without thinking of the great pile of albums that contained the record of his own childhood, and that were treasured with pride by his grandmother. No wonder Mary had burst out like that. He had never heard her speak so passionately before, and for the first time he felt he was beginning to get some idea of what went on within that dark head and unknown heart of hers. And yet, now that some sort of shift seemed to be taking place in their relationship, James found himself looking back to his routine visits of the last six months almost with nostalgia.

There had been safety in the routine. A meal prepared by Mary and an offering of flowers or chocolates or wine from James; and a chat about Grandpa's state of health or about James's work, for Mary seldom talked about herself. And then followed coffee in the sitting-room, awaiting the royal summons from upstairs. On those occasions when the old man felt well enough to receive his grandson, the brief conversation would be strictly literary and academic: No reference would be made to their relationship, nor to James's life and work.

Once he had got the hang of it, James found these little exchanges fairly straightforward. It seemed to give the old man some satisfaction to expound his views on his own work and that of his contemporaries to an informed and attentive listener, but James was under no illusion that he was awakening any spark of long-buried tenderness in that cold and rather cruel old heart.

No. The Goff Papers could come to him only through Mary, and she was spending rather longer upstairs than she usually did after such a summons. Was G. E. Goff ill? Was he dying? Had it come at last?

With a little quickening of excitement at the thought,

James walked out into the hall. The house was as silent as ever, but the sense of something stirring remained. Normally, by this time, he would be becoming restless under the constraints that the house seemed to place on him, and afraid that if he stayed any longer he might find himself making love to Mary and entangling himself irrevocably. But tonight this no longer seemed to matter. And the fact that if he stayed on here he would be letting down somebody else, a very different sort of character from Mary, didn't seem to matter either.

After only a very brief hesitation, James walked over to the telephone extension that stood on Mary's desk, leaving the sitting-room door wide open so that he could keep an eye on the lower part of the staircase.

The line was not in use. In any case, he had plenty of excuses ready if she should find out that he was making a call. He dialled a number and almost immediately a woman's voice answered.

"I'm going to be late," said James very softly. "Something's cropped up. Sorry."

The voice began to question him, but he hung up without saying another word.

CHAPTER 2

"Ah. There you are at last," said G. E. Goff.

The long head on the thin neck peered, tortoise-like, around the side of the winged chair. The table on which the supper tray had been placed had been pushed to one side and he was tapping his stick on the floor in agitated impatience.

"What is it, Father?" asked Mary. "Do you want to go to bed now?"

"Bed? Of course not. Don't be ridiculous. I want you to get out the reviews of *Last Judgement.*"

It was his final novel, published fifteen years ago. He had written nothing since then except two short articles and a lot of personal letters, which Mary had typed for him since her mother died. Most of them nowadays were addressed to strangers or slight acquaintances, a sad sign that he had outlived his friends and contemporaries.

Mary thought of this as she took the box file down from the shelf and arranged its contents on the table. It was at such moments that her sense of pity overcame all her other feelings towards her stepfather. He was so shrunken now, so small and grey, dwarfed by the great crimson armchair in which he spent his days. Sometimes he listened to the radio and sometimes he read a newspaper, but his chief occupation was to read and re-read all those tens of thousands of words written in his praise, and to work himself up into a quivering bundle of fury over the comparatively few words of criticism.

Now and then he would dictate a reply to one of these critics, many of whom were long since dead. Mary would type these replies and hand him the heavy old-fashioned gold fountain-pen that he had used for many years, and he would grip it with all the remaining strength of the twisted fingers and scrawl the famous hieroglyph.

"That should settle his hash, I think," he would say in a surprisingly firm voice before handing the pen back to Mary. He never asked whether these letters had been mailed or whether there had been any reply, and Mary would put them away in the bottom drawer of her desk. She was a careful and conscientious custodian and did not like to throw them away, but there was quite a collection of these manifestations of an old man's vanity and she worried about them quite a lot. He seldom came down-stairs to the main sitting-room, and it was extremely un-likely that he would ever search her desk if he did, but she could never be sure.

She feared his anger. He was physically helpless and dependent on her, and yet she was as afraid of him as she had always been, ever since her infant mind had first recognized the sarcasm behind words spoken, in appar-ent affection, to her mother. But mingled with the fear was a sort of shame and horror at the crumbling of his intellect. She had never loved her stepfather, but she did realize that he had gifts of a totally different dimension from those of most people, and she could not bear to think of all his faults of character being dissected by greedy and gloating scholars.

Could she trust James? This was the question that she had been asking herself ever more frequently during the past six months. She knew how much he longed to be the first to write a full biography of G. E. Goff and thereby ensure his own immortality, and her sense of justice told her that this was a natural enough desire. If anybody had a right to the Goff Papers, surely it was the old man's direct descendant.

On the other hand, she could not be sure that James would write the kind of biography of which her mother would have approved, and her mother's judgement, in this respect as in all others, was Mary's guiding light. The publication of a savagely revealing study of G. E. Goff would make nonsense of Christina Goff's own life, and sometimes Mary felt that she would rather destroy all the manuscripts and diaries and letters than have her mother betrayed in this manner.

Could she trust James? She was very much alone with her burdens and responsibilities and longed to have somebody in whom she could confide; but the only person she knew who would understand the problem well enough to advise her was a rival scholar, interested in the Goff Papers for his own sake, and it was hardly to be supposed that he would give an unbiased opinion.

Mary's own instinct was to be trustful, to persuade herself that James would never write about his own grandfather in any way that was not fair and honourable, admitting his faults but not dwelling on them unnecessarily. But Mary was suspicious of her own instincts, for the very reason that she knew herself to be inexperienced and unsophisticated, too ready to take people at their face value. And the fact that she was so strongly attracted to James, very much in love with him, in fact, made her wonder if she was the best judge in this case.

"Do you want me to stay with you, Father?" she asked when G. E. Goff was comfortably settled with little piles of newspaper cuttings on the table in front of him.

He had already begun to read, and he looked up at her when she spoke and stared blankly for a moment as if he could not remember who she was. Mary was used to this sort of thing, but this evening it distressed her as it had never done before. Her outburst to James had stirred up, or perhaps it had been the result of, deep sources of frustration and insecurity within herself. She believed that she had come to terms with the loneliness brought on by her mother's death, but seeing the blank look in her stepfather's eyes made her suddenly realize that she had not got used to it at all, and that she had been craving human contact.

James was no help. She was much too frightened of letting him see how much she cared. Besides, he brought with him a sense of the world outside the house in Chestnut Close, a sense of freedom and irresponsibility that made her own life seem even more narrow and sterile. Of course she could not expect any sort of help or support or protection from her stepfather since he was such a very frail old man, but at least he ought to acknowledge her existence; he must actually recognize her and reaffirm her own identity.

Desperation gave her strength. She stretched out a hand and laid it over the words that he was reading.

"Father!" she cried. "Do look at me! Do please say something to me."

The pale blue eyes stared at her again, and the blank look gave way to irritation. He tried feebly, with his arthritic hands, to push her own hand away, and then he said, slowly and painfully, as if dragging himself back with a tremendous effort from some other existence, "What's the matter, Mary? What is it, child?"

She felt tears stinging her eyes. The craving for affection was like a black, empty world. She was in it all alone except for this tiny thread of life in the crimson armchair beside her. At that moment she dreaded her stepfather's death more than she had ever dreaded anything in her life before. She took her hand off the page and sank down on her knees beside the chair and covered her face with her hands.

For a few moments there was silence in the room. Mary's sobs gradually eased. G. E. Goff stared straight ahead at the long lines of his books on the shelves opposite. At last he spoke again.

"Are you unwell, Mary?"

It was enough, as indeed the mere speaking of her name would have been, to restore to her the sense of her own personality.

"I'm not ill," she said, removing her hands from her face but remaining on her knees by the side of his chair. "I'm just worried, and I don't know what to do about all the people who want to write a biography of you."

"Scoundrels!" The old man trembled with excitement. "Vultures!"

"I know. Don't worry, Father. Nobody is going to have access to any documents at all unless you give your permission. I promise you!"

There was a faint smile from G. E. Goff. "You're a good girl, Mary Morrison. It's strange that your mother never wanted you to bear my name. I'd have been glad of it, you know, but she didn't want it. I never knew why."

But I know why, said Mary to herself; it was because she wanted to feel she had one thing of her very own, and that thing was me. Aloud she said, "Does it worry you, Father? I'll call myself Mary Goff if you'd like me to."

The moment she had said this she suddenly thought that there were more ways than one of acquiring the name, and panic rose in her and swamped the comforting warmth of this moment of meeting with her stepfather. She must get him to speak now; if he didn't give her a decisive word she would no longer be able to cope with James. It was almost unbearable now, this suspicion that he was interested in her only because he wanted the Goff

Papers. As time went on, the web of doubt and misunderstanding would grow tighter and tighter. There might even come a day when she might feel that she was letting James down, breaking a promise to him, if she did not hand him the Goff Papers.

And yet she was sure that she had made no such promise. It was only that when she was with James she became confused, and all the things that mattered so much at other times no longer seemed to matter at all.

"Mary Morrison," her stepfather was saying thoughtfully. "It has a good firm ring about it."

"Then that's how it's going to stay. Please, Father, will you just tell me one thing and then I'll stop bothering you and let you get on with your reading. It's about James, your grandson."

"Is he here? I don't want to see him this evening."

"No, no, you shan't be troubled with him," soothed Mary. "All I want to know is this: Do you want him to write anything about your life and work? He'd love to do so."

"No!" It came out like a pistol shot, and the distorted fingers of both hands came down on the top of the table with unbelievable force. "No. Not James. Never. Do you hear me, Mary? Never, never, never."

"Yes, Father. I understand." It was Mary who was trembling now. She got up and walked across to the shelves holding the box files and moved several of them about at random. "Of course I can't stop him writing articles about your books," she went on, "but I will certainly make sure that he never has any of your documents."

"Never, never, never," droned the old man.

Mary continued to push boxes around. When she felt that her voice and features were once more well under control, she turned round again and came over to stand near the crimson winged chair.

"I'm sorry to have had to bother you, Father, but I really did need to know. I'll leave you now. Hector will be here in about an hour."

He nodded without speaking and bent low over the papers on the table. At the door she paused and looked back at him as if making a last appeal, but he was totally absorbed in his reading.

Mary ran across the landing and into her bedroom, bathed her eyes at the wash-basin, and then sat on her bed and stared at the carpet, as if the sight of the intricate pattern of leaves and scrolls would somehow produce order and balance in her own mind.

In the last five minutes she had achieved more than she had done in the previous five years: She had at last got her stepfather to express some opinion about his literary legacy. But there was no sense of triumph or relief, only desolation at the extinguishing of those hopes that she had not, until this moment, realized she was clinging to so desperately. It now became absolutely plain to her that if James Goff knew he was not going to have access to the Goff Papers, then he would never again come to visit Mary Morrison at Number 12 Chestnut Close.

But there was no reason why James should know. Not yet. It was a matter between her stepfather and herself, and he had not authorized her to tell anybody else. And in any case, she did not even know whether he had made a will—the dealings with the solicitor, apart from minor matters, were the one area of his life from which she was excluded. Since he hated so much to be reminded of his own death, it was quite possible that he had made no will, in which case James, as his direct descendant, would inherit everything, and Mary would be powerless to do anything about it.

In that case, why should she deprive herself of the pleasure of his company—if indeed such agitation could be called pleasure—when it might turn out that she had no influence at all on the matter that was nearest to his heart?

The debate swung back and forth. Conscience and common sense told her that she had only got into this situation because she had found uncertainty intolerable, and that if she were to say nothing to James now, it would only perpetuate this uncertainty. But she persisted in finding reasons why James should not be told, and at one point resentment entered in as well. Why should she play so fair with him when he, if he was really only coming here in the hope of getting the Goff Papers, was behaving so unfairly towards her?

"If only I knew," she cried aloud, "whether Father has made a will!"

Up popped the other voice to reproach her: "There you go again. 'If only you knew.' If only you had known Father's intentions about James, then everything was going to be straightforward and clear. Well, you *do* know them now, and it's made it worse than ever."

Mary knew this voice well. It was her mother's voice, the voice of compromise and resignation and common sense. Up till this moment she had been willing to let her own actions be guided by this voice, but now, for the first time in her life, she rebelled against it.

"But you didn't always act so sensibly yourself," she cried out in her mind as if arguing with her mother. "It's no good saying I shall just have to control my feelings. How about your own feelings? If you hadn't let them run away with you when you met my father, I would not have been here at all!"

No words like this had ever passed between them during Christina Goff's lifetime. Her daughter had never given the slightest sign that she wished she could have been born into different circumstances, a different sort of life.

Mary jumped up from her bed, so alarmed by the sudden upswell of resentment and bitterness that was taking her over that the thought of facing James seemed at the moment to be the lesser of two evils. She ran downstairs and into the sitting-room without having the least idea of whether or not she was going to tell him what his grandfather had said.

CHAPTER 3

The door was open and the lights were on but James was not in the room. Mary's first thought was that he had somehow overheard or guessed what was going on upstairs and had been so disappointed that he had walked straight out of the house and would never be heard of again. Then she saw the coffee tray on the table by the settee and a moment later James himself came into the room, cheerful and smiling, carrying a plate of biscuits and hoping that he had opened the right tin.

It was the first time he had ever made any attempt to help her in any way, and to disturb the pleasant little domestic scene with an announcement that he was never to have the Goff Papers seemed to Mary downright impossible. Surely not even her mother would have expected her to say anything about it at this moment.

"Thanks so much," she said. "I'm sorry I was so long."

They sat side by side in silence for a minute, and then Mary said, "And I'm sorry I said all that at supper."

"All what?" James was smiling again. "I don't recollect that you've got anything to apologize for."

"Saying how lucky you've always been and that you can't understand what it's like not to be. I don't think that was quite fair."

"It seemed to me perfectly fair. I'm a spoilt brat and I don't think I've ever been frustrated in anything or been refused anything I wanted."

Here was her opening. Mary did not take it.

"In fact," went on James, "I've got a feeling that I'm the one who ought to be apologizing. I know you don't like me saying that it's high time Grandpa died, but I will keep doing it."

Mary turned to look at him. "You say you don't think I'm a hypocrite. Then you must surely think I'm a prig."

James shook his head. "No. Not that either."

"Then what? What do you really think of me?"

"If any other woman had asked me that," said James slowly, "I'd have taken it as an—as an invitation. But when you ask it, I know that it's a perfectly straightforward question. There. Does that give you the answer?"

"In other words," said Mary, continuing to look straight at him in a most disconcerting manner, "I am so naïve and immature that I am practically mentally deficient."

"Oh no, no!" cried James with a feeling that he was losing control of the conversation and was plunging into deep waters. "I've always thought you were very intelligent. I can't think why you never went to university."

"Father wanted me to," said Mary, turning her head aside at last, "but I could see that my mother was dreading me being away."

James said nothing; it seemed safest.

"I wouldn't have studied literature," continued Mary presently. "I would have liked to do physics or chemistry."

"It's not too late, you know."

"Yes, I know. Mature student. Open University."

"You know about the possibilities. Well then."

"I couldn't spare enough time to do the studying," said Mary simply.

James could stand it no longer. He talked for several minutes about the sheer wickedness of people who thought they had a right to take over other people's lives completely; genius or no genius, it was unforgivable, and nobody ought to be allowed to be so selfish. It was very rare indeed for James Goff to become so furiously indignant on anybody's behalf other than his own.

"Why do you have to do everything yourself?" he concluded. "There's no shortage of money. He could have a housekeeper and a secretary and a whole host of nurses and even a paid companion—"

"Would you undertake that job?" interrupted Mary.

"He wouldn't have me," replied James quite seriously.

"He wouldn't have anybody," corrected Mary. "He only likes to have me around because he's used to me and I promised my mother I'd take care of him for the rest of his life."

If James had been feeling less agitated, he might have noticed the ironic gleam in Mary's eyes, as if she was not only mocking him for his belated championship of herself, but challenging him to extend his diatribe to her mother as well. As it was, he simply had the feeling that he was protesting too much and that he was not nearly as much in control of himself as he had believed himself to be.

"I don't suppose your mother expected him to live so long," he muttered.

"Perhaps not. We're back to that again, aren't we? Father's death."

"I'm sorry. Honestly, I didn't mean to mention it."

"No, I don't think you did. It's my fault this time. I do think about it quite a lot, you know. I don't really want to spend the next five years in the same way as the last five. I'm not so inhuman as all that."

"Five years!" exclaimed James in horror.

"Hector thinks it's quite possible. Perhaps even longer."

"What the hell does Hector know about it?"

"He's a very experienced nurse, and he's with Father

every day. And Dr. Corbett thinks so too. She told me so last week."

"Five years," groaned James, gripping his head with both hands. "I can't bear it."

"You don't have to," said Mary very quietly.

He glanced up at her. There was a pause before he said, "Are you trying to tell me that you think I am only coming to see him, and to see you too, because I am hoping to get something out of it when he dies?"

"Yes. It's true, isn't it?"

"It's true that I want very much indeed to write his biography, and that to do so I shall need to have a free run of the contents of his study. But you know all this, Mary; I've made no secret of it. That was my chief motive in trying to heal the family feud. Granny didn't like it at all. It's the only time we've ever had a serious difference of opinion. As far as she is concerned, the world would be a happier place if G. E. Goff and all his works were out of it for evermore."

"It's natural that she should feel like that," said Mary calmly, "but what about you? Would you wait five years for the Goff Papers?"

"He can't live another five years. It's perfectly absurd."

"How do you propose to stop it, James?"

"Well, I'm not going to try to put weed-killer in his chicken soup, if that's what you think, but how you have succeeded in not doing something of the sort long ago, with all your opportunities, is really beyond my comprehension."

Mary laughed and James looked at her in surprise. She laughed so seldom. It seemed to change her personality completely, as if a mask had been drawn aside and something fresh and unexpected had suddenly been revealed. He had never been so conscious of this rare transformation as he was at this moment. He stared at the smiling face and it seemed to him that the faces of all the other women he had ever known were dull and predictable in comparison.

"Mary Morrison," he said with mock reproach, "you have bewitched me. You called yourself naïve and immature, but it seems to me that you are as old as Eve and as subtle as Delilah. Yes, it is perfectly true that the one attraction that this house held for me was the hope of getting hold of the Goff Papers. I don't care in the least if I never see the old man again. And before you come out with yet another of your devastating questions, I can tell you that the answer is yes: I was interested in you purely because you were the person nearest to my grandfather and most in his confidence and for that reason more capable than anybody else of helping me to realize my ambition."

"Thank you," said Mary faintly. "I thought that was how it was. I am glad to know the truth."

"The truth!" James almost shouted the words, and then glanced instinctively towards the closed door. "Don't you realize what I'm saying?" he went on in somewhat lowered tones. "Didn't you notice the use of the past tense? I said that *was* my main interest in you. I didn't say that it *is*."

"The past tense?" repeated Mary in a bewildered manner.

She had not taken in the implications of the words at all. It was as if she had been borne along this last half-hour by some instinct that had taken over her words and actions, and now it had suddenly deserted her and left her cast up, helpless and hopeless, upon a barren shore.

"Listen, Mary," said James, holding out his hands in a gesture of surrender, "I'm trying to tell you that—"

A long loud ring of the front-door bell drowned the rest of his words.

"That'll be Hector," said Mary. "I'll let him in."

James's hands clenched into fists and he looked at that moment as if he would like to strangle Hector Greenaway. But after Mary had left the room, he slowly relaxed and began to wonder whether after all he hadn't had a lucky escape. A girl who could arouse in him a strength of feeling that he hadn't even known he possessed and bring him to the point of declaring it, was not a girl from whom one could disentangle oneself when one wanted to. It was no good trying to pretend to himself that he did not have this feeling about Mary, but at least he had recognized it now and would not be taken unawares again. By the time she returned he was sitting at the far end of the settee doing the *Times* crossword puzzle.

"I'm quite sure Father doesn't want to go to bed yet," said Mary, "but Hector insists on going up. I think I'll just leave them to it."

"Two equally obstinate old men," said James. "I wonder which of them will win."

Mary came and sat beside him and they filled in a few clues together. It was as if the earlier part of the evening had never been. Then she said, "It's nearly ten o'clock. Won't you be too late to call on your grandmother?"

This was James's convenient excuse for getting away early from the house in Chestnut Close. Old Mrs. Goff lived in a luxury apartment only ten minutes' drive away, and James himself rented a flat on the other side of London, so it made sense to combine the two visits. About once in six weeks he actually did go and see her and, since she and Mary had never met or even spoken to each other, he had never feared that his deception might be discovered.

"Yes, it will be too late," he agreed, glancing at his watch.

"But won't she be expecting you?" persisted Mary.

This girl is quite intolerable, thought James, and yet I'm as obsessed with her as I am with the Goff Papers. I have got to have them both, and soon.

Aloud he said, "I never tell Granny I'm coming for certain. I only say I'll be in this neighbourhood and may look in if I've time."

"So the poor old thing makes all sorts of preparations and then sits waiting, and you don't turn up, so she just goes to bed. You really are a selfish bastard, aren't you?" said Mary.

"I thought we'd settled that earlier this evening."

"Yes, but it had never really come home to me with such force before."

"If that's your final word on me, then I'd better go," said James, getting up. "Do I take it that you would prefer me never to pollute your home with my presence again?"

Mary began to laugh. Twice in one evening. James looked at her in despair.

"Aren't we ridiculous," she said. "Like characters in a G. E. Goff novel."

"Grandpa never writes like that," cried James, outraged. "He's much more subtle."

"He does sometimes. There are passages in *Last Judgement* that are sheer bathos. Like Thomas Hardy at his very worst."

James protested violently. "What do you know about it, anyway? You admit you've no interest in literature. I didn't know you'd even read his novels."

"Well, I have. Every one, several times over. And I think he's a very great writer indeed. Streets ahead of anybody else since—oh, since Dickens or George Eliot maybe. But that doesn't mean he doesn't slip sometimes. Even the greatest have their off moments."

"Where, for instance?" demanded James.

"Here," said Mary, walking over to the bookcase that

stood near her desk and taking out the copy of *Last Judgement* from the row of Collected Works that stood on the top shelf. "Listen to this."

In a dead-pan voice she read aloud, " 'The influence of women upon the lives of men is often so much more powerful than the reverse, although it does not show up so strongly and clearly. It is a slow and secret process, like water wearing down the rock, and only when it is too late to resist and to try to counter its effects does the man realize what has been done to him. Bertram had never in his life . . .' et cetera, et cetera." Mary closed the book.

"I remember the scene," said James. "What's the matter with it?"

"It's trite," said Mary.

"It's true," said James.

They glared at each other. There was a knock on the door.

"I'm sorry to disturb you, Miss Morrison," said a high voice with a trace of a Cockney accent, "but Mr. Goff says he doesn't want to go to bed yet. He says he wants to dictate a letter, and please will you come at once."

"Good night," said James abruptly and rushed out of the house.

Hector was the first to speak. "I'm very sorry, Miss Morrison, to interrupt, but you did tell me that I must always say at once when Mr. Goff asks for you."

He was a wiry little man, with alert blue eyes. Mary was always rather uneasy in his presence, but he coped very well with her stepfather, which was more than anybody else was able to do, and it was therefore essential to keep on good terms with him.

"Thank you," she said. "I'll go straight up."

And then, because somehow or other Hector Greenaway always succeeded in making her say more than she either wanted or intended, she stopped at the foot of the

stairs and added, "We were only talking about the n
eth-birthday celebration. There'll be plenty of ti
discuss it again next week."

It was very nearly the first time in her life that sh
spoken an outright and deliberate lie, but she was
conscious of having done so, for it seemed to be part
strange new self that was taking her over and it s
out quite naturally.

CHAPTER 4

In a large untidy attic room just off Hampstead High Street a slight, fair woman in her early thirties put down the telephone, lit a cigarette, sipped at a mug of coffee, and stared at a student's essay that lay on her knee. After a few minutes she read a couple of sentences and lifted her pen as if to make a marginal comment, but put it down again without writing, and once more stared without seeing.

The telephone rang twice more, and each time she scattered cigarette ash and let the pen slip to the floor in her haste to lift the receiver. The first call was a wrong number and the second was her sister asking her to baby-sit the following evening. She agreed absent-mindedly and listened for a minute or two to a tale of domestic woe without taking in a word.

Then she said, "Sorry not to be more help, Stella, love, but I've got a huge pile of essays to mark this evening. Can we talk tomorrow?"

Her sister rang off, with thanks and apologies, but the pen remained on the floor, and a moment later the student's essay joined it there.

Paula Glenning, a lecturer in the same Department as James Goff, got up and made more coffee and wandered around the room and looked at her watch and thought about James and herself and decided that this affair would really now have to come to an end. After one failed marriage she certainly didn't want to risk another that might go the same way, and in any case James was exceedingly unlikely to want to marry either her or anybody else, since he hated the thought of being tied down to family life, and he never did anything that he didn't want to do. Up till now he had always managed to get hold of anything that he wanted, except the Goff Papers, and no doubt he was well on the way to acquiring these as well.

Hence the hasty call to say he would be late.

It would have to end. Decently and in dignity, without any scenes or reproaches. She had known exactly what he was like from the very beginning, but it had seemed a good way to cheer herself up while she sorted out her own problems.

At ten o'clock she was still firm in her resolution, and marking the essays with feverish energy. By half past ten she was beginning not to care whether James turned up or not, and at a quarter to eleven she wanted nothing in the world but to go into a deep sleep and forget about everything, and was positively hoping that he would not come at all.

James chose that moment to appear. He looked tired and strained and refused a drink and then asked if she had any China tea because he didn't fancy anything else at the moment.

Reluctantly Paula got out some cups.

"I'm sorry I'm so late," he said.

"You're breaking the rules," she replied. "Never explain, never apologize."

"Is that our rule? I thought it was a Noel Coward quote."

"It is. *Private Lives.*" Paula yawned and rummaged in a drawer for a sharp knife to cut the lemon.

"I've mucked up your evening," said James.

Paula ignored this and poured out the tea. "One or two

of our first-year students look like being very good," she said placidly.

"Oh." He peered down at the students' essays, which were scattered on the carpet around the chair where Paula was sitting. "Have you been working?"

"It's what I'm paid for."

There was a silence. Serves him right, thought Paula: I ought to have thought of this tactic before, depriving him of the pleasure of apologizing and being forgiven. But he looked so unlike his usual confident and unassailable self that after a minute or two she began to feel quite concerned about him, and also rather curious.

"How did you get on this evening?" she asked. "Any more luck with the fair lady?"

"Mary's not fair. Rather a mousy little thing."

"I thought you said she was tall."

"Did I? When?"

"When you first started on this particular treasure hunt. About six months ago. At the beginning of the summer term."

"Oh," said James. "I'd forgotten."

Again there was a silence.

"Do I gather then that the evening was wasted?" asked Paula.

"I don't know. I don't know whether I really want the Goff Papers after all."

Paula put down her teacup and stretched out a hand to touch his forehead. "You feel quite feverish," she said. "Are you getting flu?"

"I hope not. I don't think so. Sorry, Paula. You must think I'm out of my mind. I don't mean that I'm giving up the idea of writing the biography of G. E. Goff. Whatever happens, I'm determined to have the first bite at it. I only meant that I don't like the way I've been setting about getting hold of the documents. Have you ever read *The Aspern Papers?*"

"Of course. And seen all the dramatized versions."

"Well, it's the same sort of thing. It makes one feel a bit of a bastard, trying to get a girl who's lonely and unhappy to fall in love with you in order to get her to hand over the loot and without any intention of doing anything for her in return."

"Are you trying to tell me, James, that Mary Goff has proposed marriage to you and offered the documents as a dowry?"

"She isn't Mary Goff. She's Mary Morrison."

"Why?" demanded Paula.

"Because it's usual for illegitimate children to take the mother's name."

"I know, I know!" almost screamed Paula. "I meant why wasn't she ever legally adopted? Why isn't she his legal daughter and heir? It makes quite a lot of difference to your own position, doesn't it?"

"If he hasn't made a will, then I suppose I inherit the lot. But I think it's far more likely that he has made a will leaving everything to Mary. I'm only received on sufferance. He's never forgiven Granny for running away from him."

"But you don't know for sure. Have you asked Mary if he has made a will?"

"She doesn't know whether he has or not."

"That sounds to me most unlikely. She must know. It's in her own interests to know."

"Mary doesn't trouble about her own interests."

"I don't believe it. I believe she's playing a very deep game indeed. She's obviously in love with you—for which she has my sincere sympathy, although I must say I seem to be getting over it far more quickly and easily than I had anticipated—where was I, James?"

"Falling out of love with me."

"Yes, I'm beginning to think I'm within sight of a cure. But Mary Morrison! She's a very different sort of proposition from all your other ladies. She seems to have led a narrow and repressed sort of life, from what you've told me. It isn't natural. She must break out sometime."

"She must have known other men," said James.

"She won't have known anybody at all like you."

James made a grimace as he put down his teacup.

"Don't look like that," said Paula. "I haven't put poison in it."

She was feeling light-headed from tiredness, and the ache of parting, which would nag at her on and off for some time, was already beginning; but underneath it all she had a firm and solid sense of having survived intact. James Goff was one of those monumentally heartless sort of people whom anybody with any sense of self-protection would know how to avoid, and to involve herself with him at a time when she was at a very low ebb had been most unwise. She was coming out of the affair far better than she had a right to expect—not weakened, but with a renewal of her own strength.

"I don't know what to do," said James.

"You'll just have to decide whether or not to accept her proposal of marriage," said Paula matter-of-factly.

"But she hasn't asked me."

Paula raised her hands above her head. "Heaven grant me patience! Listen, I don't know whether you are out of your mind or not, but if you go on like this much longer you will certainly drive me out of mine. Do you think you could try to get a grip on yourself and tell me exactly what has been going on this evening? I want a clear, concise narrative. Stick to the facts. No speculation at this stage, please."

"Yes, teacher." James smiled at her and Paula looked

away. "It wasn't a case of Mary proposing to me," he went on. "It was I who was on the point of proposing to her, and I'd have done so if we hadn't been interrupted."

He paused. Paula was lighting another cigarette, and did not reply.

"We'd had an extraordinary sort of conversation," said James. "She more or less accused me of wanting my grandfather to die, and then she lectured me about my selfishness—you'd have liked that, Paula—and compared my pampered existence with hers. And suddenly—I don't know how it happened—I found myself thinking about her. I don't mean just thinking about her as an object to be manipulated for my own advantage, but really wondering about her, and wondering what she thought about me. And we actually started quarrelling—about a passage in one of Grandpa's novels, of all idiotic things—and then we were interrupted again, and I came away because I felt so shattered by what I had discovered about myself that I felt I needed to be alone for a while to try and digest it."

Paula got to her feet and crushed out her half-smoked cigarette and lit another.

"What had you discovered about yourself, James?" she asked in a steady voice.

"That I'd actually gone and fallen in love."

He raised his face and there was about it the radiance of one who is seeing the whole world fresh and new. The books on the shelves and the papers on the floor, and the worn carpet and the used crockery, and the red-and-white-striped curtains that covered the dormer window; and Paula herself, in her dark-blue trousers and pale-blue shirt and her shining cap of corn-coloured hair, were all part of his new vision of the world, all misted over with the amazing glory of having fallen in love.

Paula saw with his vision, and saw that it included her only as part of the overall view, and she screwed up her eyes as if the smoke from her cigarette were irritating them, and counted her breaths, and stood absolutely still and said to herself, This pain will pass, it's already unreal and in the past. And she thought about Stella and her young niece and nephew, and about her job and the strength of her own intellect, and about art and literature and music and long walks in the country, and good conversation and loyal friends, and she said to herself, These things are real; this moment is not real at all, and it will soon be over.

"You've always said you were incapable of loving anybody," she said aloud in the same unemotional, unhesitating voice.

"I know. But I was wrong."

"I see." Paula moved back to her seat. The pain had gone as suddenly as it had come. She felt more exhausted than ever, but strangely at peace, as if a burden had been shed. "I have to believe you," she went on, "and I appreciate your coming to tell me, but I don't understand why you are in any doubt as to what you should do now. Where is your problem? It all looks extremely straightforward to me."

"Actually there are two problems," replied James. "The first one is that I don't know how I'm going to persuade Mary that it's she I care for, and not just the Goff Papers."

He paused. After a little while Paula said, "Are you seriously asking me to give you advice as to how to deal with that?"

James looked a little taken aback. "No. I suppose that wouldn't be very tactful, would it?"

"What's the other problem?" asked Paula.

"How to get rid of G. E. Goff," said James.

"Why does he have to be got rid of?" Paula was puzzled. "Do you mean that he would disapprove of you and Mary getting married?"

"Of course he would. It would totally destroy his comfort. And don't go trying to tell me that he's an old man and there can't be long to wait, because he could easily live another five years or even more. Mary says so."

"Five years," said Paula thoughtfully. "Yes, that's quite a long time to wait, particularly for a man who is barely capable of waiting five minutes for anything he wants. And presumably you would have to wait for the Goff Papers too, and in five years' time you'll be getting on a little, won't you, James, and younger and fresher scholars will be catching up with you and making names for themselves. Yes, I quite see your point."

Paula looked at him and wondered whether he had heard anything she had said. The glow had gone and he was leaning forward and staring at the carpet in a brooding manner. How could I ever have loved this man? she wondered. He thinks of nothing but himself. Now he thinks he's in love and it's a new experience for him, but he's not really concerned about Mary's welfare at all, only about the effect that she has on him. Does she realize what he is like? Has she any idea what she is letting herself in for?

"At any rate, Mary will have had good practice in dealing with a thoroughly selfish man," she said aloud, feeling that she deserved to get in a word for herself after all she had had to put up with this evening. But it was wasted because he had indeed not been listening to her at all.

"Mary's got this idiotic idea that she has got to do everything for him herself," said James.

"And if you were his age and in his position, you would expect to have someone around who would do everything for you."

"What on earth are you talking about, Paula? You're not being much help, are you?"

Paula drew several deep breaths before she spoke. "I'm

extremely tired and I'm going to bed. If you don't want to go out again tonight you can sleep in here on the settee. Good night."

He stood up when she did, but seemed inclined to linger, as if he wanted to say something more.

"Good night," said Paula again very firmly. "Leave the keys on the table if you decide to go."

She escaped into her bedroom and a minute or two later heard the door of the apartment being closed. Dignity and decency, she thought, thank God. And then nothing in the world mattered except to sleep.

Sleep came, but only for a little while. During the early hours of the morning, images of James Goff filled her mind and would not let her rest. They brought a sense of pain and loss, but even stronger than that was puzzlement and even apprehension. What would James, who could not stand the least frustration, do if he was deeply in love but failed to gain his object? He would be jealous and possessive and unreasonable and in every way intolerable, thought Paula. It might not, after all, be such an enviable position to be the woman who really mattered to James.

She found herself thinking about Mary Morrison, going over in her mind everything that James had told her. It didn't amount to very much. An odd, recluse-like girl. A household drudge. But with wit enough to see through James and spirit enough to tell him so. There seemed to be some sort of contradiction here. Was that her fascination for him?

One phrase that he had used recurred again and again to Paula's mind. How to "get rid of" Grandpa. He must surely mean only that some other arrangements must be made for the care of the old man, a nursing home, perhaps, while he and Mary floated off into their dream of bliss, but it was an odd way of putting it.

Get rid of. Paula could not get the words out of her

head, and as the night wore on, they began to take on a sinister meaning. Her love affair with James Goff was definitely over, but for her own peace of mind she was going to keep track of his activities in pursuit of the Goff Papers, and the fact that they were both teachers in the same Department of English made this a not impossible task.

CHAPTER 5

Mary had been made very agitated by James's hasty departure from the house in Chestnut Close, but it did not increase her feeling of hopelessness about him. On the contrary. It had dawned on her at last, while they argued about the merits of *Last Judgement*, that her words and actions were actually having a marked effect upon James, and that his own attitude towards her had changed dramatically. He was conscious of her, he was taking her into account as he had never done before.

This awareness, and the amazing possibilities that it opened, went to her head like wine.

Mary Morrison had always been a solitary girl. Several of the girls with whom she had been at school would come and see her from time to time to have a meal and tell her about their love affairs and their problems at their jobs. And during the last few years, when she had been dealing with her stepfather's correspondence, she had come in touch with a number of writers and literary critics and librarians and book collectors; and some of them sent her flowers and books and other offerings, and invitations to social or learned gatherings, and even found excuses for calling at the house in Chestnut Close.

G. E. Goff's stepdaughter regarded these contacts as the most difficult part of her job. Sometimes he ordered her to attend one of the literary receptions in order to report back to him on the appearance and behaviour of some rising star in that particular galaxy, and Mary's shyness made these occasions an agony for her. The easiest people to deal with were those who wrote with specific requests: Would Mr. Goff give his opinion on the latest prize-winning novel? Would he head the subscription list for a writers' charity? Would he grant an interview to be broadcast as a special edition of *The World of Literature* on the occasion of his ninetieth birthday?

This last request had been made by Richard Grieve, author, critic and broadcaster, the acknowledged authority on the works of G. E. Goff. Richard was in a rather different category from the other supplicants who wooed Mary for the sake of the literary legacy that was widely believed to lie at her disposal. His public reputation as critic, debater and interviewer was formidable; not because he belonged to the abrasive and aggressive school, but because behind an air of blandness and innocence he could be so quietly deadly. Even G. E. Goff himself, who despised everybody's intellect except his own, showed signs of respect when he was talking to Richard Grieve.

Mary knew all this, but to her Richard had always behaved with great courtesy and consideration. A tall, thin, fair man of about thirty-five who looked older than his years and talked in a pleasant but businesslike manner, he treated her as if she was a sensible and businesslike person as well. Several times they had had conversations about her stepfather's work, and he had been informative and interesting, but not in the least condescending. He never flattered her, but paid her the compliment of treating her as a human being in her own right, not just as G. E. Goff's stepdaughter, and in return she told him the truth: that, as far as she knew, no decision had been taken about the Goff Papers, and that her stepfather was so sensitive on the subject that it was almost impossible to talk to him about it.

Richard had understood at once. "Please don't feel under any pressure," he said. "We'll just have to wait and see. But if you could keep me informed of any developments, I should be most grateful to you."

Mary had promised to do so, and on one Sunday afternoon the previous June, when Richard had turned up with a complimentary copy of his recent collection of essays which contained many references to the Goff novels, Mary had told him that James was now visiting the house and seeing his grandfather.

She tried to speak without emotion, to give no hint of the impression that James had, from their very first meeting, made upon her, and she was grateful when Richard said in his calm and disinterested way, "So the family feud is being patched up. I see."

No more was said about it on that occasion, nor on subsequent occasions when she saw him or spoke to him on the phone, but Mary felt that Richard did indeed see— right through to the heart and mind of James and herself and perhaps even of her stepfather as well—but oddly enough she did not shrink from the feeling that there was somebody who understood it all. It was as if Richard, by devoting himself entirely to literature, had placed himself apart from the struggles and passions of ordinary human beings and could regard them with an all-seeing but non-judging eye.

Nevertheless, in spite of this reassuring air of detachment, there could be no doubt that he passionately wanted the Goff Papers, and Mary could not help but realize that if scholarship alone was the criterion, then he had the best claim to them. But would he write the sort of biography of which her mother would have approved? Certainly he would be truthful and unswayed by prejudice, but it might well be that the truth, seen through such eyes, would be much more devastating.

True to her policy of trying to deal fairly with everybody, Mary had told James about this talk with Richard Grieve, and had noticed the immediate alarm on that expressive face.

"Are you going to hand him over the loot?" James had asked.

"It's not mine to give," she had replied. "It's up to Father."

"If he's got any sense, he won't let Richard Grieve within a mile of his study," said James. "He's a terror. Let him loose on an author and there'll be nothing left but a handful of charred bones by the time he's finished."

"But he's written quite a lot of articles about Father's work," Mary had protested, "and they aren't all that damning. He admires him enormously."

"That's during Grandpa's lifetime, my dear. Certain conventions and certain decencies have to be observed. But after the old man's death—"

Mary remembered this conversation when she ran upstairs in answer to her stepfather's summons. James's professional jealousy had been obvious, and it had brought home to her with great clarity just what a powerful weapon she would hold if indeed the fate of the Goff Papers were to be left in her hands.

It ought not to be left in her hands. She had at last plucked up the courage to ask her stepfather about James; she ought now, if she was to behave in a fair and responsible manner, to summon up the courage to ask him about Richard as well.

But suppose he were to answer, "Yes, Richard Grieve is to be my biographer"?

Mary paused on the landing in great confusion. It was not courage that was lacking now; it was desire. She seemed to have turned into two warring selves. There was the Mary who had always been guided in all things by her mother, who had sometimes rebelled against her but never believed it possible that she could live by any other lights; and then there was the Mary who had come to life the first time she saw James Goff, saw that striking and familiar face, but on a young man, not an old one.

It was this second Mary who had decided not to tell James that his grandfather did not want him to have the documents, this second Mary who was deciding that it was better not to mention Richard to her stepfather in case he might say yes; this second Mary who was shutting her ears to her mother's voice and seeing everything around her in a new and very different light.

This solid wooden door, for instance, painted cream like all the other doors on the first-floor landing and left slightly ajar by Hector when he came downstairs a few minutes ago. Ever since she could remember, Mary had felt awe and apprehension when she looked at this door. G. E. Goff's power-house of creation had to be approached with reverence, like a cathedral or a museum. Earlier this evening, when she had come upstairs yearning for some words or gestures of affection and support, this sense of coming into the presence of something remote and monumental had been as strong in her as ever. But it felt quite different now.

She pushed the door open wide and as usual was struck with pity at the sight of him, moved by the contrast between G. E. Goff the famous author and G. E. Goff the shrivelled old man. But her fear seemed to have gone completely. What were his sarcasms, after all, but a minor irritation like the buzzing of a fly? And he was so weak and crippled that if she were to pick up that cushion and hold it over his face until he ceased to breathe he would not be able to push her hands away. Had she not proved that this very evening, when she had covered with her hand the words he was reading until he was forced to speak to her?

She had done that in the grip of desperation and before

she felt these strange new stirrings of confidence and power within herself. What might she not be capable of doing now?

No harm to him, of course. That idea of the cushion had only been to remind herself of the extreme frailty of the mortal frame of G. E. Goff. But she must unlearn the habit of deference. That would be the first step towards her own liberation.

"Here I am, Father," she said in the brisk and confident manner of one talking to an invalid or a child. "Hector said you wanted to dictate something."

He gave a little grunt, and she did not think he had noticed her altered tone of voice. There was that fanatical look in his eyes that showed his mind had wandered away into its own timeless world, and he was tapping with his bent forefinger on the printed words that lay on the table in front of him.

"Silly little whipper-snapper," he said. "It's undergraduate rubbish, of course, and hardly deserving of an answer, but nevertheless the lad will have to be put in his place."

Mary, who had sat down a couple of feet away from him, craned forward to try to see what the document was that had so excited him. It looked like a page cut from the student newspaper of one of the older universities, and the date was fifteen years ago. From where she sat she could not see the name of the reviewer, and she was not sufficiently interested to get up to have a closer look.

She was forming a resolution to bring to an end this business of writing long letters that were never going to be dispatched and never going to be seen by any eye other than her own. Why should she spend her time like this? These lapses of his were certainly not going to decrease, and there would no doubt be other symptoms of senility as the months went by. Yes, Mother, she argued with Christina Goff in her mind, I know what you will say: One must humour him; it is dreadful for such an intellect to crumble, and not only must you prevent other people's witnessing it, you must also make sure that he does not realize it himself.

But I have protected him, insisted Mary, and I shall go on doing so. Only I have to protect myself as well. Why, if I don't make a stand now, I could end up by being drawn completely into this fantasy world of his. I'm not trained for that sort of thing. I'm not a psychiatric nurse. I wouldn't be able to cope with it. It's all very well for you, Mother: You had your bit of life before you settled down with G. E. Goff. But I haven't had any life at all.

"Write a letter," said G. E. Goff, "to Mister—no, to *Master*—impudent schoolboy!—to Master Richard Grieve. Spelt *G-R-I-E-V-E*. Have you got that? Address it to—"

He broke off. Mary was not conscious of having exclaimed aloud, but she must have made some sound that had momentarily diverted him from his purpose and caused the pale-blue eyes to look unfocused and bewildered.

"I've got the name," said Mary calmly. "I'm ready to go on."

G. E. Goff leaned back in his chair. The twisted fingers came together in a little knot resting on the printed page and his tongue came out a little way and moved over the thin dry lips. The eyes stared straight ahead.

Mary, recovered from her surprise and suppressing a tendency to laugh that she had never felt in her stepfather's presence before, glanced up from her notebook. It was as if she were looking at some marble bust. The mind of G. E. Goff had floated out of time and space and was fixed in its own immortality.

"Sir," said the firm precise voice, "I hesitate to question the judgement of one who has acquired a vast and comprehensive experience of life during his twenty-one years on this planet of ours, but I feel bound to point out—"

Mary wrote automatically, the mechanism of ear and mind and hand continuing to record the words, while her thoughts were free to wander. Richard Grieve. Considering how prolific a writer and critic he was, it was perhaps strange that this was the first time one of these curious epistles had been addressed to him.

But no. She realized almost at once that she herself was being guilty of some sort of misjudgement of time. The reviews over which her stepfather brooded were mostly from many years back, printed soon after the first publication of the novel in question. The only book that Richard could have reviewed on publication, unless he had indeed been writing as a schoolboy, would have been this final novel, and at that time he had been only an undergraduate student contributing to a university journal, and not the much dreaded critic that he was later to become.

It was not strange, then, that no such letter had been addressed to Richard before, but it was very disconcerting to find herself writing one of them to a living human being with whom she was personally acquainted, instead of to somebody dead or at any rate forgotten. By the time G. E. Goff had finished dictating what turned out to be an even more virulent attack than usual, Mary had made up her mind what she was going to do.

Here was her sticking point. Chance had thrown at her an excellent opportunity. She would make him understand, tactfully, of course, that his mind had these lapses. You cannot do it, it is too cruel, said her mother's voice in her mind. But it is cruel to let him be put into a position where people could sneer or laugh at him, she replied; I am going to do this; it is for his sake as well as for mine.

G. E. Goff, well satisfied with his composition, pushed the newspaper cuttings aside and shifted about in his chair as a preliminary to heaving himself out of it and preparing to be helped to bed. It was later than his usual hour and he looked very tired. Mary almost relented. What did it matter, after all, that she had wasted half an hour in writing shorthand notes that would never be used? There were many worse ways of spending the time.

In any case, he would not expect her to type them tonight, and by the morning he would probably have forgotten that he ever dictated the letter. The kindest and most sensible thing to do now would be to forget all about it. She could put the notes away in her desk without even bothering to transcribe them. This would, in a way, be her own little gesture of rebellion, and she could hear her mother's voice saying that this was the right way; that all G. E. Goff needed was to prove to himself that he still possessed the power of words, even though all other faculties were failing, and for this he needed an audience.

No, it was not so very much to ask, to spare a little time for such a purpose. Most people would not even consider it a hardship at all, but rather a privilege to listen to the sentences formed by such a mind, even in its decline. But Mary could not do it. The need to assert herself, now recognized at last after having been denied for so long, was too strong for her mother's voice or for her own sense of justice and charity.

"Father dear," she said in a patronizing manner that she had never used to him before, "have you by any chance noticed the date of this review that is agitating you so much?"

She picked out the newspaper cutting that he had put aside and laid it in front of him, holding it down firmly on the table.

"There," she said. "Just you look at that date."

It was indeed as if she were talking to a forgetful and not very intelligent child. His hands moved helplessly; her right forefinger pointed at the date as if she were teaching him to read.

"You see," she said, "it's fifteen years ago. Fifteen years. Mr. Grieve is no longer an undergraduate. He is a very well-known writer and literary critic. And in fact he is coming to see you the day after tomorrow to record an interview to be broadcast on your birthday. I don't think it would be very sensible to send him a letter like this, do you?"

Even while she was speaking she had the feeling that she was going too far, that she was not being careful and tactful at all but deliberately and cruelly insulting. She had the sense of plunging into unknown depths, but she was unable to stop herself. It was as if she could only burst out of the constraints of her whole life by taking a leap from which there was no return.

But the moment she had finished she felt terrified, both of herself and of him. She let go of the newspaper cutting and stood back, looking down at the familiar figure in the chair, hoping with all her heart that he had not taken in her meaning, that his mind was still so deep in its own world that he had not heard her.

For a moment it looked as if this hope might be justified. She saw the pale-blue eyes blinking, and then suddenly they opened very wide and in them was the bright glare of sanity; and she saw the fingers tapping on the table and the whole body writhing in impatience at its weakness; and her own mind cried out in a silent prayer—scold me, abuse me, but please say something quickly, however cruel, however unfair; say anything you like so long as it brings us back where we were before, back on dry land, however hard and unwelcoming.

And she realized then, when it was too late to turn back, that he had known all along about these lapses of his and that his outbursts of irritation were an attempt to cover them up; and he had known all along that she knew, and he had trusted her, and that was why he had never asked whether she had mailed the letters; he knew that he could trust her to keep up the pretence without which he would be like a shellfish without its shell, a human being without its skin.

He continued to tremble and to shift about in his chair and to stare at her with this terrifying look of knowledge and awareness, and she stared back in horror, paralysed in mind and will, unable to make any attempt to repair the damage that she had done.

His lips moved as if in speech, but no sound emerged, and it came to Mary's mind that he could be having a stroke, but still she could make no movement to help him.

Then the words came at last, but not in the usual clear, firm tones. His voice sounded thin and weak and very old.

"Do you hate me so much, Mary, that you are trying to destroy me? You and James together?"

"No, Father no!" she burst out. "However can you have such a terrible idea?"

She took a step forward and then stopped, not knowing what to do or to say. At that moment she would have given up all her hopes if she could have returned to where they had been two hours before, momentarily meeting each other in their thoughts of the dead Christina.

"I'm sorry," she said at last. "Very truly sorry."

And then she thought she saw a way to make some slight amends. "James knows nothing about it, nor Richard either. Nor anybody else at all. Nor ever will know."

But this time he really had not heard her. His face had turned a greenish grey and he began to cough, little short painful gasping coughs, and his fingers clutched feebly at his chest.

Mary gave a little scream and her own hands went to

her throat. The next moment she was running out onto the landing and calling down the stairs in a voice shrill with panic: "Hector—come at once! He's having an attack —I think he's dying!"

dered what would happen to the girl when her stepfather died. Most people would say it would be a well-deserved release and would give her a chance to have a life of her own at last. But Dr. Corbett had seen too many people, seemingly at the mercy of a demanding invalid, go to pieces completely when the patient died. Mary Morrison might have an overwhelming need for the structure and purpose in her life that her stepfather's presence provided. She was such an odd, lonely sort of girl that it was difficult to imagine what she would do if free to choose for herself. Presumably she would not be short of money. She might even be something of an heiress and consequently be sought after. Would she be able to cope with that sort of thing?

"If Mother had been alive," Mary was saying softly, "this would never have happened."

"What makes you say that?" asked Joan Corbett.

"It's my fault that he had this attack," muttered Mary, turning her face away. "It'll be my fault if he dies."

"Nonsense," said the doctor briskly. "How could it possibly be your fault?"

"But it is, it is. I said something to him that I shouldn't."

It was two o'clock in the morning and Joan Corbett was longing to go home, but she decided that she had better stay and hear this.

"What did you say?" she asked patiently.

"I told him," began Mary and then paused, staring at the floor. "I oughtn't to have bothered him about it," she went on presently. "I knew he was very tired, but I felt I had to know. People keep asking me about them. All his manuscripts and diaries and letters. What's going to happen to them when he dies."

She paused again, looking straight at the doctor with a hopeless expression on her face. She had fully intended to tell the truth: that in her own mind she had killed her

CHAPTER 6

Dr. Joan Corbett was a short plump woman with thick grey hair and heavy spectacles. She knew the household well, and it was she who had insisted on bringing in Hector Greenaway when G. E. Goff began to experience difficulty in washing and dressing himself. She accepted a cup of tea and sat down next to Mary on the settee in the sitting-room.

"That's all we can do for the moment," she said. "Mr. Greenaway will stay with him for the rest of the night, and I'll send another nurse along in the morning. Or we could have him in hospital for a while. I think that would be best. You could do with a break, Mary. When did you last spend a day away from this house?"

"I don't remember," replied Mary vaguely. And then, with great eagerness: "Don't send him to hospital, Dr. Corbett. I'm sure he'd hate it."

"And what about you?"

"I'd rather have him here. Truly I would. Truly I couldn't bear to think that I'd let him down at the end. I promised Mother."

"But my dear girl, you wouldn't be letting anybody down. And it probably won't be the end. He's every hope of pulling through this time and he could live for years—I've told you so before. Your mother never expected you to sacrifice so many years of your life."

Joan Corbett looked at Mary in concern. They had had conversations like this before, and she had often won-

stepfather as surely as if she had put the cushion over his head, but the words that came out were not those she had meant to say.

"You mean you had been asking him what he wanted done with them?" asked Dr. Corbett.

Mary nodded.

"And that upset him?"

Mary nodded again.

"It's perfectly natural for you to ask him," said Dr. Corbett, "and it's equally natural that he should be upset. People never like being made to think about what is to happen after their death, and the older they are, the less they want to be reminded of it. I do have some idea of your problems, you know, Mary, and I think you cope with them very well indeed. You are not in the least to blame, and you must put right out of your mind the idea that this attack is in any way your fault." She stood up. "I hope you'll feel better now for having told me. Would you like me to give you something to help you sleep?"

Mary shook her head, looking even more hopeless and wretched than before.

"I think you should," said Joan Corbett. "I'll leave two tablets, just in case."

Mary waited until she heard the doctor's car drive away, and when the silence of the night was once more complete in the house, she ran upstairs to her stepfather's bedroom.

The door was not quite shut, and she stood outside it on the landing for several minutes, longing and yet dreading to go in. She wished now that she had said nothing to Dr. Corbett. Half a confession was worse than none at all. The only thing gained, if indeed it was a gain, was the knowledge that the doctor had no suspicion of the truth.

But what of the nurse, who always made her feel ill at ease so that she said things she had never meant to say?

Hector knew a lot more about the household than the doctor did, and was probably more in G. E. Goff's confidence than any other living person, including Mary herself. Hector had seen Mary and James together, obviously deeply absorbed in each other; had seen James leave hurriedly, and would certainly suspect that the heart attack was the result of something that Mary had said. But even Hector could not know what that something was. Listening at the door would not have helped him, since sounds carried so little in this house.

She would be all right so long as she kept her head and let Hector think that she had been pestering the old man to say that James could have the papers. That would fit in with what she had told Dr. Corbett and with what Hector himself had observed, and it was understandable and forgivable, which the truth was not. That was her story and she must stick to it, and nobody would ever know what had really happened. Nobody.

Except the old man himself.

Mary stepped aside from his bedroom door and leaned against the wall to steady herself. The realization had come very suddenly and made her feel giddy.

"Are you trying to destroy me? You and James together?"

Those were the last words that she had heard him say and she could not forget them. But he would remember them too when he woke up again. There was no doubt at all that his mind had been perfectly clear when he spoke those words, so clear that it could see right into Mary's, farther than she had at that moment seen herself.

Of course he had guessed that she loved James and would do anything to hold him, and that was why she wanted him to have the Goff Papers. And of course he had connected his refusal with Mary's rebellion, and concluded that she and James were in league against him.

And the knowledge of his own weakness had made him afraid and brought on the attack. And he would come back to consciousness with this fear and this knowledge still in his mind, and nothing that Mary could do or say would ever remove it and restore his trust in her.

If only he were never to speak again. If only it had been a paralysing stroke and not a heart attack. If only she had listened more closely when Dr. Corbett and Hector had been discussing his condition, instead of letting her mind grow dim with apprehension, then she might know better now what would be needed to ensure that he never spoke again.

To destroy me. You and James together. Had James put the idea into her head? She could not remember ever having thought about it until James came into her life. But she could not help seeing that it was James's wish that the old man should soon die, and it seemed that the wish had transferred itself to her, and drowned her mother's voice completely.

Mary straightened up and pushed at the bedroom door. She had every right to go in; she was in charge of the house, and Hector had no right to send her away.

She thought at first that the nurse was asleep. He was sitting on a low chair by the side of the bed, leaning back with closed eyes. On the other side of him was a table on which was a heavily shaded lamp, a glass and a jug of water, several small bottles containing medications, and a white pottery bowl containing an assortment of dried flowers. Christina had been very fond of such arrangements, and Mary had kept them up in memory of her mother and because it seemed to please her stepfather. In front of the bowl stood a small photograph of them on their wedding day, G. E. Goff looking tall and distinguished and younger than his sixty-five years, and Christina with the nervous smile that Mary knew so well, for she had always hated being photographed or appearing on any public occasion.

Mary stood just inside the door and stared at these familiar things as if they belonged to another life. Then she looked at Hector, sitting so neatly in his chair, with hands folded in the lap of the white jacket that he always wore on duty, and the feet in the soft noiseless slippers placed side by side.

He was an old man himself, and he must be tired too after the exertions of the last few hours. But he slept like a cat, resting and yet aware of what was going on around. At the slightest change in the patient's condition he would be fully alert at once. And Mary was sure that he knew she was there and was waiting to see what she was going to do.

Silently she moved towards the bed. It was a high, old-fashioned mahogany bedstead, and at first it looked as if it had no occupant. The faint light from the lamp showed only a very slight raising of the bedclothes. When her eyes had adjusted to the dimness, she saw his face. It was like a death mask. It seemed impossible that the blood should still flow and the breath still rise and fall. And he must be heavily drugged. It wouldn't need even a cushion, it would need only the firm pressure of a hand to extinguish that tiny flicker of life.

Mary clasped her hands tightly together and stood looking down at the bed. She knew she was being watched. She told herself that she would never do such a thing, even if the nurse were not there, even if nobody was ever to find out. But nevertheless she wished that she and the old man were once again alone together.

"He looks so grey," she whispered. "Oh, Hector, are you sure he is going to be all right?"

"Doctor says so, Miss Morrison." The voice was as wide awake as if he had never been dozing at all. "Can't say I've got much use for lady doctors as a general rule, but Dr. Corbett—she's thorough. And she don't miss much."

Mary experienced a little spasm of fear. Did Dr. Corbett suspect her after all? Had they been talking behind her back, deciding that she must never be left in charge of her stepfather again?

"I think we're very lucky to have her," she said, making a tremendous effort to speak in her normal manner. "And we're lucky to have you too. I don't know what I'd have done if you hadn't been here when he was taken ill."

"I dare say you'd have managed, but I reckon it was a good thing I was here all the same."

Was it her imagination, or was there an additional meaning in his words? Perhaps she could find out.

"I don't mind sitting with him for a while if you'd like a break," she said. "I don't feel the least bit sleepy."

"That's kind of you, Miss Morrison," was the reply, "but there's not so much of the night left, and I'm used to it. It's my job. Why don't you try to get some rest yourself? You could do with it."

Mary felt no wiser than before. "Supposing he wakes up," she said, "and asks for me?"

"If he wakes up and asks for you, then I'll call you right away. Just like I always have done. But he won't wake tonight." Hector glanced at the bed. "Not with what he's got in the bloodstream."

Mary could find nothing else to say. She went into her own bedroom next door and lay on the bed dry-eyed and motionless but with her mind in a tumult. For minutes at a time she could think of nothing but how to prevent her stepfather from telling anybody about what had preceded his attack. Then suddenly her thoughts would shift and she would feel quite sure that she was worrying without cause; that nobody suspected her of any evil intent towards him; that he himself had forgotten, or at any rate forgiven, her stupid attempt to bring home to him his own infirmity. And then she was equally sure that she would never be forgiven, because she had hit at the vital spot, his pride in his own ability, the very heart of him.

He never forgave. James, whose only offence was that he was the grandson of the wife who had deserted G. E. Goff, was admitted only grudgingly, and the reviewers who dared to criticize him were savagely attacked. Nothing could ever wipe out what she had done to him. For them to live in the same house together would henceforth be impossible. Those words of hers could cost her her home; they could cost her her inheritance.

And they could cost her James.

The battle continued in her mind, shifting slightly to one side. Should she tell James the truth?

At half past seven in the morning she was awakened from a short exhausted sleep by the telephone ringing by her bed.

"Mary, my love." It was James's voice. "I'm sorry to be so disgustingly early, but I just couldn't wait any longer to apologize for my behaviour last night."

"Your behaviour," repeated Mary uncomprehendingly.

"Yes. Rushing off like that without even saying good night properly. Have you forgiven me?"

"Nothing to forgive."

"But you don't sound very pleased about it. What's the matter, Mary? Is something wrong?"

"Your grandfather had a bad heart attack last night," she said wearily.

"Good God! Is he dead?"

It was impossible not to notice the excitement in James's voice.

"He's not dead," replied Mary. "Dr. Corbett thinks he's going to recover."

"Oh." There was a silence. Then James said, "I was

going to ask if I could come over to see you this morning, since there's something I particularly wanted to tell you and I was hoping we wouldn't keep being interrupted, but if Grandpa's ill and you're very busy—"

"I'm not busy. Hector's looking after him."

"So I can come?"

"Yes, please. As soon as you like."

Mary put the phone down with the relief of having made up her mind at last. She would tell James exactly what had happened. He would have to know, and he would have to help her, because it was he who had started it all. If it had not been for James, she would never have rebelled against her stepfather, but would have gone plodding along her narrow way, clear in conscience even if only half alive.

Her reason was functioning better now and she felt more in control of herself. If she were to lose everything, then so would James. There was no way in which he could benefit by her loss. His only hope of gaining his ambition was to stick to her, now more than ever. They were entwined together and must decide together what to do.

James put the phone down in the living-room of his flat, which was not far from Paula's, and dialled Paula's number. She sounded sleepy and not at all pleased when she heard his voice.

"If you're going to ask me to forget last night's conversation and return to the *status quo ante*, then the answer is in the negative," she snapped.

"Well, actually, darling, I wasn't going to suggest that, though I admit that I'm calling to ask you to do something for me."

"That goes without saying. If it's anything to do with helping you with your lady love or with the Goff Papers, then the answer is also no," said Paula.

"It's nothing to do with either. Not entirely disconnected, I admit, but not directly to do with them."

"Okay then. Tell me the worst," said Paula resignedly.

"Could you possibly take my first-year's Elizabethan poetry class for me this morning to save me having to come into college? I don't need to be there for anything else. Would you mind very much?"

"Of course I don't mind," said Paula. "Why couldn't you ask me straight out?"

"Because I felt a bit embarrassed about asking you anything after last night."

"You're never embarrassed, James. You just wanted to test my reactions. And you also want to tell me what's happened. Paula the good old pal."

"It's Grandpa. He's had a serious heart attack."

"Good Lord." Surprise and concern. Quite different from James's first reaction to the news. "Is he alive?"

"Just. I gather they think he may get over it."

"Bad luck, James. Better luck next time."

"What on earth do you mean? I hope you're not trying to suggest that I engineered my grandfather's heart attack?"

"Of course not. But you'd be very glad to be rid of him. You said so yourself last night."

"Paula!" James sounded so genuinely horrified that Paula's suspicions began to weaken.

"I'm sorry," she said. "I suppose most of us would benefit, one way or another, by somebody else's death. But there's all the difference in the world between the wish and the deed. If there weren't that difference we wouldn't have much of the great literature of the world, including *Hamlet* and *Macbeth*."

But James was not to be diverted into a literary discussion. "You got me really worried for a moment," he said. "I'd no idea that anything I said last night could have given such an impression. I hope that if Grandpa does die, you won't go around spreading rumours that it was my doing."

"You ought to know by now that I'm not the sort of person who goes round spreading rumours," she retorted. "But I confess I was thinking it might be a good idea to keep track of you."

James groaned. "Are you jealous, Paula? I didn't think you were a jealous sort of person."

She laughed. "We haven't time to discuss it now. I've got to dig out some of my old lecture notes if I'm going to take your class, and you'd better hurry up and make sure of your Mary and stake out your claim for the Goff Papers before Richard Grieve makes his bid. He'd make a better job of the biography than you would, James."

"How did you know he was after the documents?"

"It's moderately obvious, isn't it? Besides, I happen to know Richard quite well. We got friendly after he gave that talk to our postgraduate group. No, I have never talked about him to you because I know that although you've never been in love with me, you could still be jealous. Now I've got to go. Look after Mary Morrison. I'm worried about that girl."

He began to question her further, but the line had gone dead. Serves him right for hanging up on me yesterday evening, thought Paula to herself as she dragged books and piles of papers down from the shelves, creating even worse disorder in the big attic room. She felt resentful enough to be pleased that he had reacted so strongly to her mention of Richard Grieve. In fact, now that her spare time was not to be taken up with James, it would be a good plan to get in touch with Richard, whom she had not seen for some months, exchange news, and have the pleasure of some peaceful company and civilized conversation.

Naturally she would ask Richard what he intended to do about getting hold of the Goff Papers. James must fight for himself now.

CHAPTER 7

"I don't think you've met James," said Mary a couple of hours later. "My stepfather's grandson."

"Ah, the missing heir," said Dr. Corbett. "No, I don't think our visits to this house have ever coincided, but I guessed at once who you were. The resemblance is very striking." She smiled at him warmly.

James made her a little bow. "Thank you. I only wish the likeness extended to other qualities as well as physical appearance, but then I suppose most of us who happen to have a genius as an ancestor must feel that way."

"Don't fish for compliments, James," said Mary, also smiling. "You haven't done all that badly for yourself."

He made a little gesture of self-deprecation. "I don't suppose I can be of any help here, but I had a free morning and I thought Mary might be glad of a bit of company. How is Grandpa now?"

"Better than I expected," replied Dr. Corbett. "Mary doesn't want him to go to hospital, and if he goes on as well as this I don't think there will be any need to move him. Mr. Greenaway will be back again this evening, and Nurse Lowder is with him now. She's worked for me before and she's very reliable, and I thought he would prefer somebody older rather than a young girl."

Mary left them to talk and moved towards the bay window. She looked out at the fallen chestnut leaves, golden-brown in the pale winter sunshine, and at the crimson of the late roses in the front garden, and felt within herself a great stirring of life and hope, as at the coming of spring.

Everything was going to be all right, now that James had told her that he loved her and would take care of her. She had kept to her resolution of telling him exactly what had happened between her stepfather and herself, and he had not thought it dreadful at all. In fact, he found it incredible that she had not lost patience with the old man long ago. Nobody else would have put up with this sort of thing for so long. Mary's mother? Well, of course that was different. Husbands and wives had to put up with things, or thought they had to.

James's reaction had been like balm to Mary's conscience. He had agreed with her that G. E. Goff might remember the incident when he recovered, but he did not think there was any cause for panic. Even if the old man did get over the heart attack, he would be weaker than ever and totally dependent on other people. What James and Mary had to do was make quite sure that those other people realized that the old man could no longer be considered of perfectly sound mind. This business of dictating letters to people long since dead would have to come to light, but properly presented, as it would be by James, it would not reflect discredit on Mary at all. On the contrary, it would serve a double purpose. It would show how extremely caring and loyal she was, and it would be useful evidence of the old man's senility.

"The important thing is to make people realize that he is not capable of handling his affairs," James had said. "There is nothing illegal in that. There is also nothing immoral in it, since it is perfectly true, so you can put that overworked conscience of yours to rest for good and all."

After that had come a long interval of not talking at all, and then Mary had dragged herself away at last to open the door to Dr. Corbett, and James had remained in the kitchen while the medical consultation went on upstairs, and now the important introduction had taken place and James was making the sort of impression he always did make on people at first meeting.

Soon he would be telling Dr. Corbett that he and Mary were going to get married, and the doctor would be delighted for Mary's sake, and only too pleased to help them both in any way she could. And after the doctor would come the lawyer, and no doubt he would make an equally good impression there, and nobody could suspect him of fortune-hunting—not in the commonly understood sense at any rate—since he was due to inherit a substantial sum of money from his grandmother.

Everything looked so very different in the bright light of day. The shadowy bedroom, the deathlike face of her stepfather, the weak, angry, unhappy voice in which he had uttered those words of accusation—all these seemed unreal when set against James's glowing confidence in their future. Their future together.

It was James's voice that filled her mind and heart and brought warmth and hope. Could it be wrong to grasp at this joy when you had done nothing that you should not have done, but had spent so many years doing what other people wanted you to do? The sunlight on the roses, the blackbird on the lawn, and the children who lived opposite coming out of their front gate on their bicycles, all seemed to cry out, "No, it is not wrong," and Mary almost believed them.

But still she could not quite forget two things. One of them was the look in the old man's eyes when he said, "Do you hate me so? . . ." and the other was his tone of voice when she asked him whether James should have the papers. "No, not James. Never, never, never . . ."

She had still not mentioned this second incident to

James. If she told him about it, would he be able to reason away her guilt?

Surely she need not put it to the test just yet. Surely she had the right to float a little longer on this great wave of wonder and joy.

"I'll have to go now, Mary," said Dr. Corbett, "but I'm leaving you in good company."

Her broad face was beaming. She's happy because she doesn't have to worry about me any more, thought Mary. But Hector said the doctor didn't miss much. Then why doesn't she see she's being used? Mary asked herself irritably as she made a suitable reply. For a second or two she longed for Dr. Corbett to suspect and to accuse her of having caused her stepfather's illness, as if that alone would be her salvation. Then her mind shifted focus again and she knew once more that James's way was the only way.

"Is it all right for me to go in and see Father?" she asked.

"But of course, my dear. It's your home. You've cared for him all these years and I know you'll take care not to excite him."

She sounded surprised at being asked the question, but Mary was staring at her with dark eyes very wide and lips trembling, as if she was crying out for help.

"Oh, I see." Dr. Corbett glanced at James, who gave a barely perceptible nod. "You're still worrying about that little upset you had with him yesterday. Well, of course you won't try to talk any business matters with him until he's a lot stronger. And even then it may not be too easy. We may well find that his mind is a little confused when he recovers consciousness."

"Yes," said Mary, "I suppose we may."

She had the sensation of a trap closing around her. Where was the joy of a few minutes before? It would come back, of course, as soon as the doctor had gone and she and

James were alone together, but she would still be in the trap, imprisoned by her own happiness.

And so it turned out. Even the postman delivering a parcel and the milkman collecting the week's money took on something of the rosy glow; little commonplace events were transformed because she was sharing them with James. The trap was still there, but its walls were blurred and at a distance.

Halfway through the morning she said, "I think I ought to go up and see Father now. I'll take Nurse Lowder a cup of coffee. That'll be a good excuse."

"Shall I come too?" asked James.

"No. Better not." She gripped his hand convulsively. "It won't make it any easier. Sorry, darling. But you do understand?"

"Mary." He held her back a moment. "You mustn't be too disheartened if he doesn't speak to you at all. It doesn't mean that he's holding any grudge. How often has he completely ignored you or been offensive for no reason at all, even when he was quite well?"

"That's true," said Mary. It was wonderful how James could always say the right thing to reassure her, to keep her safe within the trap of joy. "Kind words from Father have always been few and far between, but it didn't really matter because I knew I'd done nothing wrong. But this time—"

"You've done nothing wrong," said James very firmly. "You've put up with him with the patience of an angel, and in a moment of great stress it slipped slightly. Which shows you are only human, and I for one am glad of that." He kissed her again. "Very glad of it. I used to be scared of you, Mary. You were such a paragon of truth and virtue."

"Not really." She managed a smile. "Only nervous and shy. Let me go now and get it over. I'll try not to be silly about it, but if I come down in floods of tears please bear with me."

"Don't forget Nurse Lowder's coffee. We want to keep on the right side of her. One never knows when it will come in useful."

It was Mary's own thought, but she would rather not have had it expressed at that moment. The door of her stepfather's bedroom was now much more alarming to her than the door of the study had ever been. The nurse had left it slightly open—perhaps she too suffered from the claustrophobic atmosphere of the house—and Mary could see the end of the table with the bowl of dried flowers and the photograph taken on her mother's wedding day.

It gave her courage, she had a right to be here. Nurse Lowder was not unlike Dr. Corbett in manner and appearance, and she seemed to be a most competent and enthusiastic knitter. Mary admired the intricate design of a sweater as she placed the coffee cup on the table. There was no sign of sound or movement from the bed.

"Is he asleep?" asked Mary in the same low voice that she had been using up till now.

"He dozes much of the time," replied the nurse, "but he was quite lively a little while ago. I'm sure he'll be pleased to see you." She stood up and laid a hand on her patient's wrist. "Are you awake, Mr. Goff? Here is your daughter come to visit you."

Mary stood a few feet away from the bed, reluctant to go any nearer. The old man was propped up against the pillows, and although he still looked very pale, the ghostlike quality had gone from the face. His eyes were shut and he did not open them when he spoke, slowly and clearly, emphasizing each word in turn.

"I—have—no—daughter."

"Oh dear," said the nurse, looking distressed. "I think

his mind must be wandering again. He's had rather a lot of drugs."

"He's quite correct," said Mary quietly. "I am not his daughter."

"But my dear—"

"Don't worry." Mary interrupted the nurse. "I don't think he wants to talk to me at the moment. I'll come back again later."

She walked out onto the landing and the nurse followed her.

"I'm so sorry, Miss Morrison. This sort of thing happens sometimes when people are very old and confused, and families can be very upset about it."

"I'm not upset, Nurse. I quite understand. Don't forget I've known him nearly all my life."

Mary felt frozen. It was no effort to speak calmly, but after her last words she sensed a slight lessening of sympathy towards her on the part of the nurse, as if the latter was thinking, that's a cool one, not much feeling there. My first big test, thought Mary as she walked slowly down the stairs, and I've failed it. I ought to have confided in Nurse Lowder—nurses love to chat—and told her that my stepfather had become confused and that I was afraid he might have taken offence at something I said in all innocence. James would have said something like that; James would not have been cool and remote; James would have handled it properly.

But James was not waiting for her in the big sitting-room. She looked for him in the dining-room, a dark, rather gloomy room that was never used nowadays, and then in the kitchen, but there was no sign of him. Perhaps he had gone out into the garden to get some fresh air. Mary walked across the lawn and looked behind the shrubs at the far end before returning, increasingly anxious, to the house.

At first she had not been altogether sorry to have a minute or two to collect herself before telling James what had happened, but now she was beginning to wonder whether he had changed his mind about her and had run away. Was all that wonder and glory nothing but a dream?

Of course she knew that it was real, and yet she had a few moments of paralysing panic before it occurred to her that he had probably only gone upstairs. She ran up again, longing to call out his name but not daring to for fear her stepfather might hear, and reached the top stair just as James came out of G. E. Goff's study.

Mary stifled another cry, caught hold of the hand he held out to her, and they went downstairs together. Then the threatened flood of tears began, and James was comforting and indignant with his grandfather for making her so unhappy.

"It's not his fault," she muttered. "He was almost asleep and hardly knew I was there."

And now I am lying to James too, she told herself, and while he continued to murmur soothingly, her thoughts went round and round in a narrowing spiral of despair. Why had he been to the study? Why had he not told her he intended to? Why such haste? She really had believed him when he assured her that he loved her for herself alone. During those incredible minutes he had seemed transformed, scarcely recognizable as the man whom her mind had often criticized, even while her heart was so entrapped. But if he could not wait even a few minutes to have a look at the treasure he craved—

"I've been rather wicked," said James as if reading her thoughts. "I was thinking that it might be helpful, when we see the solicitor this afternoon, if we could show that we knew something of what he intended to do with all his possessions, and it occurred to me that it might be a good idea to have a look in his desk. I'd have suggested that we have a hunt round together, but I was afraid you wouldn't want to go rummaging in the drawers."

"I never open them unless he tells me to," said Mary, half-reassured, half-apprehensive.

"There you are. I was quite right. It needed somebody unscrupulous like me."

"Did you find anything?"

"Shall I tell you?" he asked teasingly. "Aren't you afraid it may burden your conscience still further?"

"Please, James. Don't laugh at me about it. I can't find it funny at the moment."

"I know, love. I understand. Here it is." He pulled a folded piece of paper out from his jacket pocket. "In the top drawer of the desk, pushed right to the back."

"This must have been written some years ago," said Mary, studying the paper. "It's a long time since he's been able to write as clearly as that."

"But you agree that it looks as if he was thinking of making a will and was jotting down some notes about it. Would he do that sort of thing?"

"Yes," replied Mary slowly. "He always used to make brief notes about anything he proposed to write. I think this must have been written soon after Mother died. That was probably what made him think of making a will. Or altering it. But of course we don't know whether he ever actually executed it." She glanced down at the paper again and read from it aloud. " 'House—Mary. Plus investment income. Charities'—there's a query after that. 'Manuscripts and diaries, et cetera'—a whole string of queries after that, and then on a new line underneath he's put 'BURN THEM' in capital letters."

She handed the piece of paper back to James and said, "Do you know, darling, that is exactly what I've sometimes wanted to do myself."

James looked horrified. Then he relaxed and said,

"That's not fair. If I'm not allowed to be joking, then you mustn't be either."

"I'm not joking. I've seriously thought of it."

"But the documents are part of the national heritage! You might just as well talk of blowing up Westminster Abbey or sinking the Crown Jewels in the mud at the bottom of the Thames!"

"I'm not responsible for Westminster Abbey or the Crown Jewels, but I might well find myself responsible for the Goff Papers," she retorted.

"Not if I can stop it. Not if you feel that way about them. For Christ's sake, Mary, will you promise me not to do anything drastic, whatever the provocation?"

"I promise not to destroy any document whatever."

"I hope I can trust you. I'm seriously wondering whether it's safe for me to leave this house."

She did laugh then, not quite in the way that so enchanted him, but near enough to it to convince him that she was entirely his; and Mary told herself again that everything was going to be all right; that James had given excellent reasons for searching the study without asking her consent, and that his concern about the documents was quite natural.

For a little while the joy returned. And then yet again she remembered her stepfather's cry: "James is never to write my biography—never, never, never."

And the trap closed in on her again and she could see no way out. Never.

CHAPTER 8

"Why not come and have lunch with me when you've finished your morning's teaching," said Richard Grieve to Paula on the telephone. "Then you can praise my cooking and admire what I've done to the flat since Liz cleared out."

"She's really gone? I'm sorry, Richard."

"My own fault. I'm impossible to live with. So I've been told."

"I've been told that too. But then I know I'm incredibly untidy."

"And I go too far in the opposite direction. One o'clock then. Thanks for calling, Paula. It's brightened my day."

Richard's flat comprised the ground floor of a Georgian terraced house in one of the smaller squares in Bloomsbury, and Paula remembered it as full of abstract paintings and angular furniture, always much too hot and with nowhere comfortable to sit. She was sad, but not entirely surprised, that the marriage had not lasted. Liz was an artist, a lively and gifted girl twelve years younger than her husband. The clash of temperaments must have been uncomfortable.

"It's like a very exclusive London club," she said as she came into the vast room with its long windows looking out onto grass and plane trees. "The sort that only admits females into a tiny room on the second floor."

"Do you like it?" asked Richard.

"Enormously. What wonderful armchairs. And Cruikshank cartoons. It's just the right setting for you and your books and I hope you will eventually be happy here as well as comfortable."

"Thanks, Paula. Now I'm going to fetch our lunch. We're each having a trolley-load of soup and assorted salads. Do go and look at books if you want to, but please, I beg you, put them back in their proper places and not on the floor."

Paula laughed. "I will control myself. I will be very good. Promise."

How different is the private person from the public, she said to herself as she wandered along the shelves, holding her hands behind her back so as not to be tempted to create chaos amongst Richard's possessions; he's not the least bit frightening when you get to know him. A very restful sort of person, in fact, and even rather sad in a way, and in need of comforting.

"Did you know that G. E. Goff has had a heart attack?" she asked when they had exchanged literary and academic gossip and had reached the cheese-and-fruit stage of their meal.

"I didn't know," said Richard. "When did it happen? Is he very ill?"

Paula explained.

"I'm glad you've finished with James Goff," was Richard's first response.

"So am I. What is Mary Morrison like? You have met her, haven't you?"

"A number of times, but I still know very little about her. She's rather beautiful in a dark and brooding way, but she behaves like a Victorian governess. Prim and correct."

"Hidden passions? Jane Eyre?"

"Probably, though I doubt whether Jane Eyre would have fallen for James Goff."

"What have you got against James?" asked Paula curiously.

"Jealousy," he replied with a faint smile. "He collects any woman he wants to, and he looks mighty like collecting the Goff Papers as well."

"And he is jealous of you because he knows he'll never be anything but an intellectual lightweight in comparison. But you are in the stronger position because you don't really want to collect a whole lot of women, and I don't see why you shouldn't have first bite at the Goff Papers. Have you ever mentioned it to the old man?"

Richard shook his head. "Wouldn't be tactful. One senses that there would be a tantrum."

"Nor to Mary?"

"She knows my wishes. She has promised to keep me informed."

"She won't keep that promise. Not after James has swept her off her feet," said Paula.

"I fear you are right."

Richard got up to remove the remains of their lunch. Paula watched him carefully stack the plates, neatly brushing crumbs from one to the other, and found herself coming to a resolution. When he returned from the kitchen she said, "May I smoke?"

He produced cigarettes and a very large glass ashtray which she held in her lap.

"I wish you would let me try to help you get hold of the Goff Papers," she said. "I don't quite know how, but maybe we can think of something together. No, I am not just trying to get my own back on James because he's thrown me over. I've never been under any illusions about him, either as a lover or as a writer and scholar. It's perfectly obvious, and must be to everybody who knows anything about it, that he will make a horrible job of his

grandfather's biography, and that you will make a superb one."

"Thank you. But nevertheless James has a very good claim. He's a direct descendant and he is a scholar. And nobody can prevent him in the long run from making capital out of his grandfather's reputation."

"Oh, let him spend the rest of his life writing sloppy and gossipy books about G. E. Goff," cried Paula. "But you have got to be the first, the standard biographer. Grieve and Goff go together, like Boswell and Dr. Johnson, or Mrs. Gaskell and Charlotte Brontë."

"I must admit I'd always hoped that would be the case."

"Then you've got to fight for it, Richard. What's the matter with you? I've always thought you were a fighter under that non-combatant manner of yours."

"I don't know. I suppose losing Liz has been a bit of a blow. I'm sorry, Paula. I didn't invite you to lunch to bore you with my problems."

"It doesn't bore me. I just wish I could help."

Paula waved her hand about in her eagerness, and the ash from her cigarette began to detach itself. She moved her hand and shifted the ashtray to try to catch it, but was too late. She exclaimed in horror, then glanced up at Richard, and they both burst out laughing at the same moment.

"I'm sorry," she said, peering over the side of the chair. "Would you like me to go and fetch the vacuum cleaner?"

"Don't move," said Richard, getting up from his chair. "Stay there."

For a second or two Paula thought he really was going to fetch something to brush up the tiny fragments of ash, but he came over to where she was sitting and asked her to hand him the ashtray. Wonderingly she crushed out her cigarette and did what he asked. Richard checked to make sure that every spark was extinguished, and then

very deliberately emptied the contents of the ashtray onto the Persian carpet.

Paula watched him, fascinated. When the ashtray was empty he handed it back to her with a little bow and said, "Continue. I will not interrupt your smoking again. Let the ash lie there on the carpet at least until we have drunk our coffee. I cannot promise not to avert my eyes from it, but that you will just have to forgive."

He made another little bow and returned to his seat and picked up his coffee cup. Paula looked at him with a smile of delight.

"There's a noble gesture!" she cried. "Greater love hath no man than this—that he struggles with his tidiness obsession in order to please a friend."

"A friend well worth pleasing."

There was a moment's silence and then they both spoke at once: "Where were we before that interruption?"

"Chasing the Goff Papers," said Paula. "How do we start?"

"I was supposed to be going out there tomorrow to record an interview," he replied, "but presumably he won't be fit for it."

"Has it been cancelled?"

"I've not been told so. Perhaps Mary has forgotten about it."

"Then there's your excuse," said Paula. "Don't wait till tomorrow. Pretend you've got the date wrong, pretend you know nothing about the heart attack, and just turn up there today. This very afternoon. I don't suppose you could take me with you," she added wistfully.

"I can and I will. We'll think out a reason for your presence when we're on the way."

But the tube train was too noisy and uncomfortable for conversation, and when they emerged at the other end Paula looked around her with interest, for she had been brought up in this part of London and had not revisited it for many years. So instead of discussing the business in hand, they exchanged memories of childhood, and arrived at Chestnut Close in what felt like a remarkably short space of time.

"Don't let's bother with excuses," said Paula as they walked up the garden path. "If James is still here, he'll know exactly why I've come."

"And he'll know that you've told me about the heart attack. So we'll just have to be calling to inquire how the old man is."

"They'll take it as a declaration of war," said Paula while they waited for the bell to be answered. "I'm feeling dreadfully nervous." She felt for Richard's hand and held it tightly.

But they were confronted by no more alarming figure than a middle-aged woman in a blue nurse's uniform.

"Miss Morrison isn't in," she said in reply to Richard's question. "She has gone out with Mr. Goff. Young Mr. Goff, I mean. On some urgent business, I believe."

"Have you any idea when she will be back?"

"I'm afraid not."

Richard glanced at Paula as if seeking her advice. She smiled at him encouragingly.

"I wonder if Miss Morrison has forgotten," he said. "I have an appointment to see Mr. Goff. The old Mr. Goff. I'm not exactly a close friend of his, but I am quite an old acquaintance. Could you please tell him that Mr. Grieve is here and very much hopes he is fit to see him?"

"Mr. Grieve," repeated the nurse, looking closely at Richard. "Haven't I seen you on a television programme? Ah, I know. *Watch Your Words.* Am I right?"

"Quite right. Do you like the show?"

"It's very clever," said Nurse Lowder. They were all

three now inside the house and she was shutting the front door. "And sometimes very funny."

"It's fun to be in," said Richard.

"But I don't like the way you snub each other," said Nurse Lowder unexpectedly. "It sounds very unkind."

"I'm sorry," said Richard humbly.

The nurse glanced up at him for a moment, saw what looked like a genuinely contrite expression on the pale angular face, looked a little embarrassed, and said, "I ought not to be talking to you like this, Mr. Grieve. It's very rude of me."

"Not at all," he said. "I'm interested to hear your opinion."

Encouraged by this mild reaction, she began to quote examples of what she meant, climbing the stairs as she did so, with Richard following her.

"I'll just go and see if Mr. Goff would like to see you," she said when they got to the top. "If he does, then you must only stay a little while, because although he is improving he is still extremely weak and not fit for much talking."

"Thank you," said Richard, behaving as if he had never had any doubt that he was going to be admitted, but mentally blessing the television panel game for making it so easy.

Downstairs, Paula wandered around the big sitting-room, looking with interest at the photographs on Mary's desk. There had been no need to explain her presence; it was hardly believable that things should have gone so smoothly. She was standing by Mary's bookcase, about to take out the copy of *Last Judgement*, when she heard Nurse Lowder's voice addressing her.

"Would you believe it, Mr. Goff actually recognized Mr. Grieve at once and was very pleased to see him. I don't think it can do him any harm to have a visitor. You don't think Mr. Grieve will say anything to upset him, do you, Mrs.—"

"Glenning," replied Paula. "I teach English literature. In the same Department as Mr. Goff's grandson, James. And you are—"

"Jane Lowder. All you clever people! I'm going to make tea for them. Would you like some too?"

"I'll come and help you," said Paula.

In the kitchen they searched together, both strangers to the house, for tea and biscuits and cups and saucers, calling out amicably to each other as they found things, and finally settling down into a comfortable gossip about the household.

"I've never met Miss Morrison," said Paula, "but I know James admires her very much. You don't find many girls nowadays who are willing to devote their lives to looking after old people at home."

Mrs. Lowder agreed, but Paula sensed a certain reserve when she added, "I suppose she'll get her reward one day."

"An inheritance, you mean? She will have deserved it. I gather the old man hasn't been too easy to cope with."

"So they say," commented the nurse, "though I can't say that I've found him a particularly difficult patient." She picked up the tray. "I shan't be long."

A minute later she came back full of smiles. "Would you believe it, he's actually sitting up and talking! My patient, I mean. And he doesn't look any the worse for it."

"And what is Mr. Grieve doing?"

"Sitting by the side of the bed with a pen and a little notebook and listening to Mr. Goff. They didn't take any notice of me, so I left the tray on the chest of drawers and came away."

"He'll be taking notes for the radio programme to be broadcast on Mr. Goff's ninetieth birthday," said Paula. "It ought to have been recorded, so that listeners could hear his voice, but of course he won't be strong enough for that."

"His ninetieth birthday!" exclaimed Nurse Lowder. "Of course I know that he's very famous."

The tea and chat continued to the great satisfaction of both parties. Paula felt she had learned quite a lot by the time the nurse got up reluctantly and said that she really must interrupt them now, or she would be in trouble with Dr. Corbett.

After she had gone, Paula quickly washed up, expecting every moment that Mary and James would return, steeling herself for the encounter with James, dreading it, and yet at the same time feeling that it would be something of an anticlimax if she and Richard got away from the house without such a meeting.

But their visit ended as smoothly as it had begun. Mrs. Lowder assured Richard that her patient was none the worse for having had company, and he assured her that the people who took part in the television literary panel game did not really feel "snubbed," but were quite capable of standing up for themselves; and Paula said that she was sorry to have missed meeting Mary Morrison, but she hoped to do so on another occasion.

They walked in silence to the front gate, shut it carefully behind them, and stood for a moment among the fallen chestnut leaves in the roadway, looking at each other speechlessly but with great meaning.

Then Paula glanced in the direction of the main road at the end of the cul-de-sac and her expression changed completely.

"That's James's car. Do we stay and confront?"

"No," said Richard with unwonted firmness, grabbed her by the arm, dragged her across to the opposite side of the road and said, "Don't look up. Pretend we're deep in conversation."

"They've seen us," muttered Paula, looking down at her feet as they hurried away.

"Let them make the first move then."

"This is ridiculous." Paula was inclined to giggle. "I feel as if we're in a third-rate movie."

"Keep going, girl. We're nearly at the corner."

The old Morris M.G., which James felt was better suited to his personality than a new sports car, stopped at the gate of Number 12 and its occupants turned their heads to stare at the couple shuffling along hurriedly under the trees at the other side of the road.

"We must look terribly guilty," said Paula.

"Doesn't matter."

They reached the main road. A bus was just pulling up at the stop near the corner.

"Come on!" cried Richard, and Paula found herself being hustled to the front of the vehicle, which contained only a few passengers.

"Where's it going?" she asked rather breathlessly.

"I haven't the slightest idea. I didn't see the number."

"Richard!" Her laughter broke out freely at last. "Have you and G. E. Goff been swigging too much whisky? I've never known you like this."

"We had nothing but tea," he replied, "but I do feel rather drunk. That's why I didn't want to stop and talk to James and Mary. I couldn't wait another minute to tell you."

Suddenly he sobered down, took her hand and raised it to his lips, and said, "It's all your doing. One day I may be able to thank you."

"What's all my doing?" demanded Paula.

"Fares, please," said a voice above their heads, and they looked up to see a dark face surveying them with interest.

"Oh," said Richard, and turned back to Paula. "Where are we going?"

"Where are *you* going?" she asked the young West Indian.

"Heaven," he replied, rolling his eyes upwards.

Richard produced a pound note. "Two at fifty pence, please," he said, "and could you kindly tell us when our money has run out."

The conductor tore off the tickets and walked away shaking his head.

"Now," said Paula, settling herself comfortably in her seat. "Tell me everything."

CHAPTER 9

"Who is the girl with Richard Grieve?" asked Mary. "Do you know her?"

"Yes," replied James slowly. "She teaches in the English Department at college."

If Richard had been alone, thought James, he would have stopped the car and called out and asked him to come back to the house for a little while, because it was just as well to keep on good terms with your rival for as long as possible.

Richard could be trusted not to say or do anything outrageous. It was Paula who was unpredictable, and it had been a considerable shock to see her there. James did not think it very likely that she would let him down in front of Mary, but he could not be quite sure. In any case, he did not feel in the right mood for what could be a very awkward encounter. The visit to the lawyer's office had not been as satisfactory as he had hoped.

"We ought to have spoken to them," said Mary as she got out of the car. "I'd quite forgotten to let Richard know about Father not being fit to be interviewed. He's had a wasted journey. No wonder he wouldn't look up."

"He's no right to be annoyed with you," said James, thinking that he really must get Mary out of this habit of always blaming herself, "but I agree that he didn't look as if he wanted to stop and talk. In any case, I thought you said the appointment was for tomorrow, and not for today."

"I thought it was, too, but I must have got it wrong."

They came into the house. "I suppose I'd better go up and see how Father is," said Mary. She glanced at James. He looked tired and dispirited, and for the first time since she had known him she had the impression that he was not completely in control. "No, I won't," she said. "First of all I'm going to make you some tea. Go and sit down."

But when she returned from the kitchen a few minutes later, he was wandering restlessly about the sitting-room. "I suppose it couldn't be somewhere in here," he muttered, picking up the china dogs on the mantelshelf and peering into their hollow interiors.

"Father's will? If he's made one. No, I shouldn't think it could be in here, darling. Mrs. Gordon dusts very thoroughly, and every now and then we have a big clean-out and move all the books and the furniture. It'll be in the study, if anywhere."

"Have you got keys to all the cupboards and filing cabinets?"

Mary walked over to her desk and pulled open a little drawer. "They're in here," she said. "The little keys are the three filing cabinets. The larger keys are the cupboards, and then of course there is all the stuff on the open shelves—the box files containing reviews and articles about him, and those piles of black notebooks on the high shelf near the door are the diaries. I expect you noticed all this when you were hunting for the will."

"Yes," said James.

Try as she might, Mary had not quite been able to keep the note of reserve out of her voice, but she told herself that it was no use feeling resentful towards James. She had known all along what he wanted; she still believed—she had to believe it since it was all she had to cling to—that he truly cared for her; and she had now committed herself so far that she was in no position to deny James the thorough search of G. E. Goff's possessions that he was obviously longing to carry out.

Yet the thought of it was very distasteful to her. If only they could have waited a few days until her stepfather was stronger and she had had a chance to make her peace with him, for that was what she believed she had now decided to do. She would not go along with James's attempts to show that G. E. Goff was not entirely of sound mind; she would go to her stepfather with a sincerely contrite heart and beg his forgiveness. Only if he continued to reject her would she be obliged to fall in with whatever plan James suggested, because after all it was her own fault that she was no longer G. E. Goff's nearest and most trusted companion. If she had not forfeited the old man's trust, she would now be in a far better position to help James achieve his desire. Instead of which she was in danger of herself becoming a disinherited heiress.

Mr. Howard Guthrie, the elderly senior partner with whom Mary had corresponded on a number of minor legal matters, had received them courteously and appeared to think it quite natural, in view of G. E. Goff's state of health, that they should want to know whether he had made a will.

Unfortunately he had very little information to give. After the untimely death of Christina Goff, he had strongly urged Mr. G. E. Goff to make a will, otherwise his stepdaughter would inherit nothing.

"He had always assumed," added Mr. Guthrie, addressing Mary, "that your mother, being so much younger than himself, would outlive him, and in that case, of course, she as next of kin would have inherited if he had died intestate, and in due course you yourself would have inherited through her."

This confirmed what Mary and James had worked out for themselves, but did not get them any further. Mary had been glad that James did not mention the piece of paper from the drawer in the study and that he seemed well able to control his own eagerness when talking to the old solicitor.

"Am I right in thinking," he had asked, "that if my grandfather does not recover, and that if no will is found, then I am the sole heir?"

Amidst a great deal of ponderous jargon Mr. Guthrie informed them that this would probably be the case, but added that of course he could only speak for his own law firm when he said there was no will. It was perfectly possible that Mr. Goff had instructed a different solicitor to act for him in this matter, or even that he had executed a document himself; such documents, if correctly signed and witnessed, being valid legal instruments, although not very satisfactory from a professional point of view. No, Mr. Goff had never mentioned that he was thinking of doing any such thing, but, as they all knew, he was a very independent-minded old gentleman, and there was no knowing what he might have done.

"Have you ever thought," James had asked tentatively at this point, "that my grandfather might be—er—might not be quite so clear in his mind as he used once to be?"

"He has never shown any sign of mental confusion in his dealings with me," said the lawyer firmly. "Very much to the contrary."

After this, even James had not had the temerity to hint at signs of senility again.

They had driven home almost in silence. There had been no reason to hope for anything definite from this interview, and yet it had been disappointing. Many things were possible, nothing was definite, and they were both of them, in their different ways, craving for certainties. Seeing Richard and Paula leaving the house had made the uncertainty even worse for them both, but neither of them seemed inclined to talk about the visitors. Mary was wondering whether James was better acquainted with Paula than he had implied, and James was wondering whether Mary might perhaps know of some promise made to Richard about the papers but didn't want to tell him.

They drank tea in silence. Then James stood up. "Let's go and have a search for the will now," he said. "We'll feel better if we're actually doing something about it. This whole business is beginning to get on my nerves."

"On mine, too," said Mary.

Her morning's joy seemed to belong to another life. At that moment she could not picture any sort of happy future for herself and James. Despair must have communicated itself, for the next moment they were holding on to each other as if each were the other's lifeline, and James was begging her to forgive him, and saying that he did truly love her for herself and not for her inheritance, but if she realized how much it meant to him; and she was saying that she did realize, and that of course she believed him, and they clung together more closely.

Nurse Lowder had to knock on the sitting-room door twice before either of them heard her, but she was not aware of any awkwardness because she was feeling rather flustered herself.

"I heard you come in," she said to Mary, "and I meant to come down at once to tell you that we had visitors, but I had to attend to my patient, and then I was afraid that all that talking might have been too much for him after all, although he seemed to enjoy it so much, and I thought I'd better sit with him a little longer to make quite sure he was none the worse, but he's fast asleep now, and I do honestly think it's done him all the good in the world to have that little chat with Mr. Grieve, who really is the most kind and considerate . . ."

During this rather breathless narrative James and Mary had exchanged glances of horrified realization, unnoticed by the nurse, and had then hastily fought to get themselves under control.

Mary was the first to succeed. "Just a minute, Nurse Lowder," she said with commendable calmness, "we saw Mr. Grieve and his companion walking away from the house, and assumed they had been calling here, although we didn't actually speak to them. I'm afraid I forgot to tell Mr. Grieve that my stepfather was ill and wouldn't be able to see him, but I assumed that you had done so when he came to the door. Do you mean that he has actually been in the house, that you actually took him upstairs to talk to my stepfather?"

It was impossible for Mary to keep the alarm out of her voice as she spoke these last words, but the nurse put her own interpretation on it and became even more apologetic.

"It was very wrong of me to let him in, and truly I don't quite know how it happened, except that he said that you had arranged with him, Miss Morrison, to have an interview with Mr. Goff that was to be broadcast on his birthday, and he seemed so friendly and unassuming—and his friend too—and I felt sure he would leave immediately if it seemed to be upsetting my patient in any way, but on the contrary it seemed to cheer him up, and Dr. Corbett will be coming to see him soon, and I'm sure she will agree with me that—"

By this time James had recovered himself enough to take over.

"Mrs. Lowder," he said with a fair approximation to the manner he assumed when he wanted people to think how charming he was, "nobody is accusing you of anything. You are taking wonderfully good care of my grandfather, and if you say he's come to no harm, then I'm quite sure he hasn't."

Nurse Lowder visibly calmed down and suggested that James might like to come up and see for himself.

"All right," he replied after a quick glance at Mary. "If you are quite sure that he's fast asleep. I don't think he knows I'm here, you see, and I wouldn't want to give him a shock. I'll just take a peek at him and come away."

"I left him asleep," said the nurse, "but I'll go on ahead and make sure."

"Don't worry, darling," James whispered to Mary. "I won't let him see me. But I'd like to have a look in his bedroom. I've never been in there."

"Just as I thought," murmured the nurse a moment or two later. "Sleeping like a baby."

She looked at her patient with great satisfaction while James quickly assessed the contents of the room. Heavy old-fashioned wardrobe and chest of drawers; some bookshelves, tables and chairs; and of course the bed itself. Plenty of places to hide an envelope or some sheets of paper. Looking for a possible will was not going to be a quick and simple task, even if carried out without interruption after the old man's death, let alone when being done surreptitiously.

His glance finally came to rest upon the head on the pillow. The nurse was quite right. There was an air of peace and serenity about it that was quite absent from G. E. Goff when he was awake.

"Has he been looking like this all the time he's been ill?" whispered James as he and the nurse moved out onto the landing.

"I've only been with him today," she replied, "but this is the most peaceful I've seen him. A lot of the time I thought he was rather restless and agitated."

"Perhaps I ought to have come up before," said James. "Maybe what he needed was to talk to someone."

"I think that's right," replied the unsuspecting Mrs. Lowder. "He was talking away to Mr. Grieve. You wouldn't have thought he'd have the strength."

"What were they talking about? I believe they have great literary discussions," added James with a smile.

"I think I heard Mr. Grieve say, 'It's a fine book but not your masterpiece,' or something of the sort, so I suppose they were talking about his novels."

James felt only slightly reassured. "Were you with them all the time?" he asked.

"Yes," replied the nurse too hastily. Then she added, looking rather guilty again, "No. Tell a lie. I went down to the kitchen to make them some tea, and I gave some to the young lady as well. I do hope Miss Morrison doesn't mind. I felt it was rather making free with somebody else's kitchen, but on the other hand, I had been left in charge."

By the time James had chatted a little longer to Mrs. Lowder, working hard to soothe her down again, he had formed a pretty accurate notion of what had been going on downstairs, at any rate, during the visit, and his feelings towards Paula were far from charitable.

"I don't think there can have been any drafting and signing of wills," he said to Mary, who had begun in a rather desultory way to prepare a meal, "because you need two witnesses to the signature, and the witnesses must not inherit. So that cuts out Richard as witness, and I'm quite sure Mrs. Lowder would have said so if she had actually put her signature to anything. So unless there has been yet another person in the house, which seems very unlikely . . . All the same, it is most unfortunate that one of us wasn't here."

"It was you who wanted me to come along to the solicitor," Mary pointed out.

This was true. He had not liked her talk about burning manuscripts and letters, and had felt it would be a good idea to keep an eye on her until the whole situation had become clearer. But nothing was clear at all. Mary herself was as fascinating to him as ever, but she was becoming more and more of an enigma, and he was beginning to suspect in her a much greater capacity for independent thought and action than he had realized. His grandfather, who had seemed for the time being at any rate too weak to pose any threat, and who, James had genuinely convinced himself, was on the borderline of senility, was not only gaining strength physically, but was also showing himself beyond all doubt to be in full possession of his intellectual faculties. And Richard Grieve, by some stroke of ill luck—or was it by intention?—had turned up on what James was convinced was the wrong day, whatever Mary might say about it having been her mistake. While, as for Paula . . .

For a moment or two his mind raged impotently at Paula, and then he was suddenly struck by an idea. Obviously she and Richard were plotting together to get hold of the Goff Papers, and it rather looked as if they might have won the first round. But James would turn the tables on them, if he could carry out the scheme that was forming in his mind. It must be done while Nurse Lowder was still on duty and before Hector Greenaway arrived for the night, since he was a much tougher proposition than the rather sentimental middle-aged nurse. And it must be done while Mary was busy in the kitchen.

"How long are you going to be?" he asked her.

"We can eat in about twenty minutes' time," she replied. "Is that all right?"

She seemed preoccupied too. And she was chopping

mushrooms and collecting other ingredients for some kind of rice dish, which didn't look the sort of meal that one could dump in a pan and safely leave on the cooker to look after itself. Five minutes might be enough for his purpose—ten, at the very outside.

"Then I'll go and get my case out of the car," he said, "and take it up to the guest-room, if you're quite sure that it's all right for me to stay overnight."

Mary glanced up from the kitchen table and smiled at him. "I'm glad you're staying. It makes me feel better."

"Darling!" He waved a kiss at her and hurried away.

Chestnut Close was not very generously provided with streetlamps and there was nobody about; but in any case, thought James, it doesn't matter if anybody does see me take a suitcase out of the car. That was the easy and legitimate part of the proceedings. He had left the front door of Number 12 slightly ajar, and he was careful not to shut it completely when he returned, because leaving the house for the second time must be as noiseless and swift as possible, with no unnecessary unlatching of doors.

The main guest-room was on the second floor, above the study. On his way up James noted that the study door was open, but that the old man's bedroom door was now closed.

That was lucky. He was moving very silently in this silent house, but nevertheless, if the door had been open Mrs. Lowder might have become aware of his presence and come out to say something. One and a half minutes since he had parted from Mary in the kitchen. The next five would be the crucial time, but he had his explanations ready if interrupted at any stage of the operation.

CHAPTER 10

"Everybody out," said the conductor.

Paula and Richard had been so absorbed in their talk that they had not noticed it had grown quite dark and that the bus was now empty but for themselves. They looked up and saw through the windscreen in front of them the brightly lit interior of a huge shed.

"Where are we?" Richard asked the young West Indian as they all got off.

"North Croydon bus depot," he replied with a wide grin. "You've had your money's worth."

And he hurried off in the direction of the canteen.

"We'll have to find a taxi," said Paula in a worried voice as they stood at the edge of a most unpromising stretch of road, with a long row of hoardings on one side and a blank high wall encircling a gasworks on the other. "I'd no idea it was so late," she went on. "I've promised my sister I'd baby-sit. She and Don have got opera tickets, and I've just got to get back in time."

"Where does she live?"

"Near Regent's Park."

Paula thought she saw a cab, stepped into the roadway, and then hastily jumped back as a huge truck appeared from nowhere and threatened to annihilate her. "It's hopeless here," she said unhappily as the tide of commuter cars coming out of Central London rolled remorselessly on.

Richard took her arm. "We'll go back to the bus depot.

There must be a phone-box somewhere, or else somebody will have to take pity on us and let us make a call."

But it was another twenty minutes before they were at last sitting in a minicab, and the Pakistani driver set out on what seemed to be a most circuitous route for a north-bound vehicle. Paula looked at Richard in despair.

"I'll ask him," he said. "I feel very bad about this. It's my fault you're so late."

The driver assured them that he knew what he was doing. They always contacted the police helicopter, he said, when they had to get through the West End traffic in the rush hour, and he'd been advised to keep away from Regent Street and Piccadilly. Chelsea Bridge would be their best way over the river.

He was a young man and he spoke English with a strong London accent. In the glare of lights at a big crossroads Paula and Richard looked at each other in hopeless resignation.

"They all think we're lovers," muttered Paula, "with no way to be alone together except on public transport."

Richard nodded and then said ambiguously, "I think he's got it right. Just a minute."

He leaned forward and spoke to the driver again. Paula leaned back in the cab and shut her eyes. At this moment she would have liked to be alone, quietly digesting all the events of the last twenty-four hours and praying that she would not be letting Stella down.

Richard seemed to sense her mood. "I've asked him if he can wait when we get there and take two people on to Covent Garden. He's all right. He says he'll make it in time. Let's try to relax now."

Paula shut her eyes again. Sometime later she opened them to look out of the window and see the string of lights on Albert Bridge.

"I'm conscious once more," she said. "Do you want to

be put down anywhere? I don't want to drag you out of your way."

"I don't mind coming to Regent's Park and I'm eager to see the outcome of this particular piece of the drama. Just look at that traffic," he added as the driver inched his way through the congestion on the Chelsea Embankment. "I'm beginning to feel quite guilty towards James. He deserves some of the loot if he's willing to drive through this several times a week in pursuit of it."

"We're not there yet," said Paula soberly. "Not by any means."

"Are you referring to your sister's home or to my taking possession of the Goff Papers?"

"Mainly the latter. I've been thinking it over and I'd say this afternoon has put you on equal terms. But you don't know James."

"But Mary—"

"Mary's in love. That makes her not quite sane, and capable of anything. Do you mind if we don't talk about it any more until we get to Stella's? I have got to sit on the edge of the seat and concentrate on hating the driver of every vehicle in front of us."

"I'll say no more," said Richard. "Enjoy your torment."

He kept silent for the rest of the drive, occasionally glancing out of the window, but more often looking at the tensely hunched shoulders and the restlessly moving bright golden head beside him, with an expression very different from anything that those who knew only the public personality had ever seen.

"Camden Court," said the driver, triumphantly pulling up to the curb.

Through the swinging doors rushed a taller and darker version of Paula, followed by an equally anxious-looking man.

"Take the cab!" cried Paula. "He knows where to go.

Introductions later," she added, waving a hand in Richard's direction. "Kids all right?"

"In bed asleep. Help yourself to eats and drinks."

"And add my tears at Violetta's death," said Paula. But a second later she had turned round again to thrust two 10-pound notes into her sister's hand. Stella began to protest, the driver hooted impatiently, and Stella's husband cried, "For God's sake let's go!"

"You're going to need it!" Paula shouted after them. "We've come a long way."

The ground-floor apartment was small and crowded but tidy and clean. Richard looked around approvingly.

"The twins are fast asleep," said Paula, returning to the living-room. "With any luck they'll remain so."

"If you'll show me where everything is," said Richard, "I'll cook you a meal."

"But you gave me lunch."

"That was a long time ago. I'm famished. Aren't you?"

"It seems so odd, you being here," remarked Paula as she opened cupboards in the kitchen. "It isn't exactly your scene."

"Isn't a change of scene frequently recommended as a cure for heartache?"

"G. E. Goff," said Paula firmly sometime later. "Let's have another look at your notebook."

Richard produced the little black-covered notebook in which he had written several sentences at the old man's dictation. Paula read them aloud.

" 'I, George Ernest Goff, of Number 12 Chestnut Close, London South-East, being of sound mind, hereby state that I wish Richard Francis Grieve, of 22 Fitzherbert Square, London W.C. 2, to take into his possession after my decease all my manuscripts, diaries, letters, and other documents; to make what use of them he wishes; and to keep them for as long as he wishes; and finally to deposit them in a library of his own choosing.'"

"Followed by a recognizable authentic signature," said Richard. "Of course it isn't a legal will. We've already decided that. But it's a valid statement of intent."

"It's a pity that the nurse and I weren't there to witness his signature," said Paula.

"Believe me, I did think of that, but in the circumstances I could do nothing. He was in such a state of agitation while he was dictating this that I was afraid he could have another heart attack any moment, and he only managed to sign it through sheer will-power. And I was somewhat agitated myself by that time, thinking that Mary could return at any moment, and the best policy seemed to be to hold on to what I'd got. And I don't think what I have got is worthless," added Richard, taking the notebook back and pocketing it.

"Heavens, no. It's wonderful. As I said, it brings you up to even chances with James. You wouldn't have had a snowflake's chance in hell without it. How to make the best use of it, that's the problem."

They were silent for a minute or two, and then Richard said, "I was thinking about that in the taxi, and wondering whether it wouldn't be best to tell Mary about this straight out. Whatever her feelings about James, she surely can't ignore such a plain statement of her stepfather's wishes."

Paula frowned. "I don't like it."

"Why? What harm could it do? I'm not going to hand over this document. Legal instrument or not, I'm going to guard it with my life."

"I'm not worrying about any harm to your cause," retorted Paula. "I'm worried about G. E. Goff himself. If James gets to know that he wants to bequeath you his papers, then I wouldn't give much for the old man's chances of surviving to make a new will."

"Am I understanding you correctly?" asked Richard. "Are you saying that James wouldn't stop at murder?"

"I don't know," said Paula unhappily. "I agree it sounds quite mad. But I can't forget that sort of menacing impression I had when he was talking about getting rid of G. E. Goff. Most of me keeps saying that he isn't that sort of a villain, and then I imagine him in a position where he actually could get rid of G. E. Goff without anybody else ever knowing, and I just can't see him resisting the temptation. I only hope we haven't gone and precipitated something by going there this afternoon."

After a moment's thought Richard said, "I certainly had the impression that the old man was quite disproportionately glad to see me. If we have got to speculate, then I would guess that he did not trust anybody around him very much. And I would also guess that he looked much calmer and stronger by the time I left because he believed he had not only disposed of his papers in the way he wanted, but had also removed the motive for anybody to try to remove him."

"But he must have realized that this document isn't legally binding?" pointed out Paula.

"I'm not so sure. He was weak and the circumstances were stressful. And it may have more force than we realize. I'll have to get professional advice."

"I'll go and peep at the infants," said Paula, "while you sit and think. Only another hour to go. I'm beginning to feel that today has been going on for a very long time."

When she came back to the living-room, Richard said, "Would your sister mind if I use her phone?"

"Go ahead. D'you mind me overhearing?"

"I want you to. Is that Mary Morrison?" he said a moment later. "Richard here. I'd like to apologize for this afternoon. It was extremely rude of me not to stop and talk when I saw you returning home, and I have no excuse except that I felt it would not be a comfortable or convenient meeting for any of us at that moment."

He paused and listened. Paula could not hear what was being said at the other end of the line.

"Thank you, that's kind of you," said Richard. "Actually I'd had rather a shock myself. First of all, finding that your stepfather had been so ill, and secondly, I was extremely surprised by what he told me. . . . Yes, he was indeed very much awake and wanting to talk to me. I wasn't able to record an interview, of course, but he made a few comments that I'd like to use in the broadcast. And if he continues to gain strength, perhaps I could come back in a day or two to get some more material? . . . Tomorrow? . . . Was I supposed to be coming tomorrow? I definitely had it in my mind as Thursday. . . . It's Wednesday today?"

Paula, watching Richard closely, smiled and nodded and mimed applause. She had guessed what he intended to do.

"Your stepfather told me something this afternoon," Richard was saying in a serious voice, "that pleased me enormously but came as a great surprise. I don't know whether he has said anything to you recently about his papers. . . . Then I'm afraid it may come as a bit of a shock to you too, but I hope you will be pleased, or at any rate not too displeased. I understood from him that he is bequeathing me the entire contents of his study . . . yes, he has already signed a document to that effect."

Paula applauded silently again, but Richard was not looking at her. He was staring at the telephone as if it were in some way offensive to him. He doesn't like doing this, she thought; he's sorry for Mary and he feels as if he's cheating her, but he knows that if he doesn't do this, she is going to cheat him, and much more seriously.

The telephone conversation continued for some time.

"I don't know how to convince you that I am not making all this up," said Richard at one point. "The whole business came as a complete surprise to me. . . . Naturally I am very pleased. You know this has long been my wish, to write the biography of G. E. Goff, and when the time comes, which I hope will not be just yet, I shall do my utmost to produce something which he would have approved of. . . . I am sorry that you are disappointed. I rather feared you might be, but I can only repeat that I have made no attempt whatever to influence your stepfather's choice."

There was silence while Richard listened. Paula watched his hand moving restlessly along the back of the settee, and the expression of distaste on his face grew more marked.

"I can say no more," he said at last. "I can only repeat what I've already said. Your stepfather told me, entirely of his own free will, that he has taken action to ensure that the Goff Papers come into my possession when he dies. If you still suspect that this is some kind of confidence trick, then I can only beg you to refer to your stepfather himself. Perhaps he will tell you more of the details than he has told me."

Another short silence. Then Richard said, "James? No, I have said nothing about this to James. That is why I didn't tell you about it earlier. I wanted to speak to you personally. Yes, I can well imagine how disappointed James will be. I should have been equally disappointed had I heard that the papers were bequeathed to him. You must use your own judgement about whether or not to tell him. . . . Isn't he with you? . . . Yes, it is getting rather late. I expect he'll soon be back."

The telephone receiver was replaced at last. Richard twisted round on the settee and held out his hands to Paula. She gripped them hard, saying, "Well done."

"I feel a swine," he said.

"You had to do it. There's nothing gained by her not knowing. What was that about James not being there? I thought he'd moved into Chestnut Close permanently."

"Apparently he announced about three hours ago that he would call on his grandmother, since he was in the neighbourhood, but Mary sounds as if she doesn't believe that's where he's gone."

"Poor girl," said Paula. "She probably suspects that he's gone to see me. He couldn't pretend that he didn't know me, and she must have been very curious." She yawned. "Here come the opera-goers. I'm afraid we'll have to listen to their raptures for a little while."

It was nearly half past one in the morning before Paula at last got back to her attic flat. The day had indeed been a very long one, but instead of letting her coat fall in a heap on the floor and dropping her shoulder-bag on her desk so that its contents spilled out, which was her usual procedure when coming home late and tired, she took the trouble to find a coat-hanger, and removed the lecture notes that she had been using that morning and put them in a tolerably neat pile on a shelf.

She smiled to herself as she did so, remembering Richard's heroism in deliberately spilling cigarette ash on his carpet, and wishing he could see her own efforts at reform. This weekend I'll have a big clean-up, she promised herself, and as she glanced around the room, assessing what would need doing, she noticed the keys lying on the coffee-table, next to an overflowing ashtray and a plate containing some soggy-looking biscuits.

Paula picked up the keys—one for a mortise lock, one for a Yale—and frowned at them. They looked like the keys to the main entrance to the house and to her own apartment at the top, but she could not understand how they came to be lying there, and she was a little worried, because she was usually careful about keys and things that really mattered.

Then she remembered. It was the spare set that she had given to James, and when they parted she had told him to leave them on the table. She really ought to have picked them up before she left for work in the morning, and put them in the center drawer of her desk, but she had been in an even greater hurry than usual, looking for the Elizabethan poetry notes.

Relieved at having discovered the explanation, Paula dropped the spare keys into the desk drawer, shut it firmly, undressed and got into bed, and was almost instantly asleep.

CHAPTER 11

Mary put down the telephone receiver and let despair take her over completely. Richard's call was only the culmination of an evening that had brought ever-increasing frustration and anxiety. James had suddenly become cheerful and chatty while they were eating their meal, but instead of reassuring her, this made her suspicious because she felt sure that he was hiding something. Then she had asked what seemed to her a few perfectly natural questions about Paula, and his voice had taken on a teasing and patronizing note, making her appear naïve and ignorant as well as jealous, and she had protested accordingly.

Of course there had been an immediate reconciliation. Mary was learning already that James was very good at apologizing and being forgiven—but the temporary return of something approaching happiness was short-lived. Dr. Corbett arrived to see how her patient was getting on; Hector Greenaway appeared soon afterwards to take up his night duty, and James announced firmly, when they were all four of them in the sitting-room, that he felt he was in the way and that he'd take the opportunity to pop over and see his granny and would be back later.

This did him no harm with Dr. Corbett, who was very much taken with James, and Hector kept his thoughts to himself; but it deprived Mary of the chance to speak to James alone, which might have helped her to assess whether he really did intend to visit the old lady or whether it was an excuse to go somewhere else. And Dr. Corbett's announcement, made after consultation with Nurse Lowder, that Mr. Goff was making an excellent recovery, forced Mary into the position of pretending a delight and relief that she did not feel. It would have been much more comfort to her to hear that her stepfather was not expected to last out the night; but on the other hand she knew that if the doctor had said this, she would feel more guilty than ever, so tightly was the trap of her circumstances closing about her.

But through all the comings and goings she had continued to hold fast to her resolution to seek a reconciliation with her stepfather. If he would forgive her she felt that she could bear anything at all.

Anything. Even losing James.

But the moment she had decided this she knew that she could not bear losing James, because for all the anxiety and conflicts and difficulties that he was bringing her, he also brought her the warmth that she had always craved and never known, and, having once glimpsed it, she did not think she could live without it again.

Nevertheless she would speak to her stepfather. Maybe it would go some way towards repairing her shattered conscience. She had actually been on the way upstairs when the telephone rang, having taken a long time to screw up her courage, but after the talk with Richard she sat for a while staring at nothing.

Of course she believed him. Of course she had known in her heart, even before her stepfather had said, "Not James, never . . ." that Richard was the one whom G. E. Goff would trust most. She had only made those protests, of which she had felt ashamed even while she was uttering them, because she felt James would have wanted her to.

She knew there was no hope now. Some part of her was

even happy in its despair. At least she had the satisfaction of knowing that her own attempt to frustrate her stepfather's wishes by keeping quiet about them had not succeeded. Richard would have his just reward, and James would have to cope with his disappointment as best he could. He would probably not desert her, because he valued too much what people thought of him, but there would not be much of joy in a life with a disappointed James.

When Mary at last roused herself to go up to talk to her stepfather, it was with the courage of total hopelessness. The trap had closed upon her for ever. All she could do was to make her conscience as comfortable as possible inside it.

G. E. Goff, freshly washed and shaved and looking quite pink and lively, was propped up against his pillows with a book open in front of him, and Hector was arranging the lamp so that he could see the pages.

"There you are, chief," he was saying. "Very different picture from this time last night, ain't it? Hullo, Miss Morrison. Just telling your old man how much better he looks. Not finished yet. Oh no. Not by a long chalk."

Mary approached the bed. Her hopelessness seemed to have lent her a clarity of vision, and she saw G. E. Goff as if in double focus, both viewpoints equally true and equally clear. There was the human being of genius, and there was a self-centred, bad-tempered old man, who to her had always been old; who had ruled her own existence and stifled all joy in it, and whom she now knew that she had never loved. Perhaps, in a sense, she had actually hated him; hated him because she knew they did not really belong to each other; because he was not the man whom her mother had loved; because he looked after her from duty and not from love. And he had always known that she felt this way, but she had not known it herself because her mother had worked so hard to prevent her from knowing.

None of this seemed to matter now. She had done him a grave injustice when she sneered at his forgetfulness and she was determined to tell him that she was sorry for it.

"Father," she said firmly, "may I please talk to you alone?"

G. E. Goff stared straight at her and did not answer at once, but she believed that he saw what she was seeing and had understood. Hector straightened himself up and Mary could both see and feel the little man's hostility to herself. But it no longer had any effect on her.

"There's something I very much want to say," she went on. "If you are not fit to talk, then of course it will have to wait, but Dr. Corbett said you were very much better."

"Yes, I am," said G. E. Goff. "Leave us alone, Hector. I'll ring the bell if I need you."

The nurse gave an exaggerated shrug. Neither took any notice of him. He made a great show of rearranging the water-jug and medicine bottles on the table and finally left the room, muttering to himself.

"Sit down, Mary," said G. E. Goff.

"I'd rather stand. I've come to say I'm sorry. I said something unforgivable to you and I don't expect to be forgiven, but all the same I am very sorry and I wish with all my heart it had never happened."

For a little while the pale-blue eyes stared at her, cold, hard, and as interested as if they were examining a laboratory specimen.

"Yes," he said at last, "I dare say you do wish it had not happened. But since you were determined to make a fool of yourself over my grandson, it was perhaps inevitable. I am leaving my papers to Richard Grieve. You know that?"

"Yes, Father."

"Does James know?"

"Not yet."

"Are you going to tell him?"

"Of course."

Another silence. "And I suppose you think he'll still stand by you," said G. E. Goff at last. "I always thought you had more sense, but it seems that you are going the same way as your mother."

Mary, who had been perfectly calm up till then, felt every muscle tensing at the mention of Christina.

"What do you mean by that?" she demanded, taking a step nearer to the bed.

G. E. Goff did not flinch, but his hand stretched out to grasp the bell, which needed only the slightest pressure for Hector to hear it and come running.

"Perhaps I ought not to have said, 'Like mother, like daughter,' " he said coolly, "but rather, 'Like father, like daughter,' since it must be from him that you have inherited the seeds of violence."

Mary moved across to the chair in which Hector had been sitting and gripped its back. "My father was not violent," she said between her teeth.

"Who told you so? What do you know about your father?"

Mary made no reply.

"Nothing except what your mother told you," went on the old man in the same cold, dispassionate tones. "She told you that he was an Air Force pilot. A hero. That theirs was a brief whirlwind romance before his plane crashed."

Still Mary did not speak.

"I would have been quite content to keep up the deception," continued G. E. Goff, "but you yourself have chosen to tear aside the merciful veil of fantasy. If you insist on forcing truth upon others, then you must be prepared for others to do the same to you. Your father was in the RAF. Yes, that is true. But he was no hero. He was a drunken lout. There was no brief whirlwind romance. There was a sordid liaison extending over several years, during which time he frequently beat her up. When he learned that she was pregnant he attacked her with even more abandon than usual and in self-defence she tried to hit back. Her pathetic efforts made no mark, but luckily he tripped and fell, knocking his head on a heavy brass doorstop. Had he been attended to immediately, it is very possible that he might have survived, but she took herself off to the kitchen of the small house which she was renting and made herself tea. By the time she returned to investigate, he was in a deep coma, and he died on the way to hospital.

"No blame ever attached to her, and I do not think she ever felt at all guilty. Certainly she had no cause to feel so, but she judged it advisable, nevertheless, to leave the town where she was then living, and came to London to make a fresh start. A charitable institution helped her through the period of your birth, and the rest of the story, her struggles to keep you both, and her eventual arrival on my doorstep in answer to an advertisement for a housekeeper, has, I believe, been correctly related to you."

G. E. Goff had been staring straight ahead during the latter part of his narrative and had not noticed that Mary had sunk down into the chair. When he did see her, his expression did not change at all but he pressed the bell.

"I am perfectly all right," he said to Hector a moment later. "It is my daughter who is not feeling well. Will you attend to her, please?"

And he picked up his book and began to read.

Fifteen minutes later James Goff let himself into the house, pleased with the way his little scheme had gone so far, and confident that Mary would soon forgive him for returning so late.

Hector met him halfway up the stairs. "Miss Morrison has gone to bed," he said. "She's not feeling well."

"Not well?" echoed James rather stupidly. It had never entered his scheme of things that Mary should not be ready at any moment to welcome him. "What's the matter with her?"

Hector gave his little lift of the shoulders. "Overtired, maybe. I've left her a couple of sleeping tablets. I don't know whether she's taken them."

"I'll go and see," said James. "I'm staying here tonight, by the way."

"That's good news," said Hector. "One patient at a time is quite enough for me to deal with."

Sarcastic little blighter, said James to himself as he knocked on Mary's door; it'll be a good thing when we can get rid of him.

Mary's bed was opposite the door. The lamp was on and her eyes were open and staring in James's direction, but for the first few seconds he could see no sign of recognition in them. It was as if she looked straight through him and beyond him, and what she saw gave her no joy. That air of mystery about Mary, which was the first thing that had attracted him to her, had never been so strong as at that moment; but at the same time he felt alarm, as if confronted with something beyond his comprehension, beyond his power to deal with.

As he hesitated, some sign of awareness came into those fathomless dark eyes, and the next moment he was on more familiar ground.

"Mary, my darling, what is the matter? I shouldn't have left you so long. But it was rather important. I'll explain later. What is it, my love? Are you truly not well?"

For some minutes he continued in this manner, while she clung to him, speechless and dry-eyed. Then she said in her old prim, reserved tones, "I'm sorry to be so stupid. You must be very tired. I'll be all right now."

"You aren't all right at all and I want to know what's the matter," said James very gently.

"Nothing," replied Mary. "It's all been . . . rather too much for me, I suppose."

"What have you been doing? Did you go in to see Grandpa?"

Her reaction was an uncontrollable shudder.

"I suppose the old bugger's recovered enough to be as beastly as ever," he muttered. "What did he say? Won't you tell me, love? It'll make you feel better, truly it will."

But still Mary could not speak.

For over an hour he persisted. For the first and perhaps the only time in his life there was no thought of self in his mind. Nobody who had ever known James Goff could have imagined him capable of such infinite care and patience.

It met with only partial success. At last Mary began to weep a little and James caught the words "my mother."

"Your mother?" he said. "Was my revolting grandfather saying anything offensive about your mother?"

There came a louder burst of sobbing.

"Your mother was absolutely wonderful," said James. "My granny has always said so."

He expanded on this theme for a little longer, and then suddenly he had an inspiration.

"Was he having a go at your father as well?"

This time Mary's weeping became almost hysterical, and for some time there was no question of any talking.

Eventually James said, "You must try not to let him upset you like this, my darling. *You* know what matters, *you* know the truth, and it's only playing into his hands to listen to his vicious lies."

She drew back a little when he said this, and for a

moment he had the extraordinary impression that in the midst of all her tears she was going to laugh. But it must have been his imagination, he thought, because the next moment she was clinging to him again, and he was trying to get her to tell him exactly what G. E. Goff had said, and saying over and over again that she would feel a lot better if she could only bring herself to confide in him.

"I know," she muttered, "but I can't say any more. Not just now. Please don't ask me. Please."

"All right, my love. Try to rest a little now."

"Yes, I'll try," she said obediently, but for many hours she lay weeping in his arms.

At last, worn out himself, he slept, and woke to the dim daylight of a misty November morning and the sight of Mary standing beside him with a tray in her hands.

He tried to rouse himself and make a little joke. "You mustn't pamper me like this. It's a bad beginning to our life together."

She made no reply, but set down the tray on the dressing-table and left the room. James, feeling dazed and stupid, drank some tea, ate some biscuits, tidied himself up a bit, and went downstairs to find Mary sitting at the kitchen table, staring straight ahead with that same look in her eyes that had alarmed him the night before.

"I didn't expect you down so soon," she said.

"I'm teaching this morning," he replied. "I'll have to leave in half an hour."

"Oh yes. Of course." It was as if she had completely forgotten that he had a job, so shut away was she in this world that nobody else could enter.

"Don't get up," said James. "I'll scrounge for myself."

But she rose as if to prepare a breakfast that he knew he was not going to be able to eat.

"Mary," he cried, catching hold of her hands, which felt

icy-cold, "you can't go on like this. We must get some help for you. Shall I stay and speak to Dr. Corbett?"

"No, you must go to work. You've taken enough time off already."

She released herself and made toast and coffee. To please her he made some attempt to eat.

"I don't like leaving you in this house," he said. "Would you like to go to my flat for the day? No, perhaps not," he added as she did not respond. "You'd be alone and in a strange place. How about coming to college with me? You could make yourself quite comfortable in the common room, or read in the library, and I'd join you whenever I could. Oh damn," went on James as Mary still said nothing, "I've got to go to this bloody reception this evening for our new Head of Department. I'll never be forgiven if I stay away. But it ought to be over by eight. It's just one of those days. But I'll cancel the lot if you need me. Mary, my dearest Mary, let me try to help you. Tell me what I can do."

He was sitting at the big deal table, as he had sat so many times before, and as he finished speaking she came round to stand beside him and he looked up at her. Her face was transformed, glowing and transparently alive as it was when she laughed. But she was not laughing now. She took his face between both hands and held it upturned towards her and bent and kissed him and said, "Thank you, James. I don't think you'll ever know quite how much I thank you. You have comforted me very much. Try to remember that. Please try always to remember just how much you have comforted me."

"And will do so again, I hope," he said, trying to speak lightly. "Though I hope too that there aren't going to be so very many occasions when you need comfort. I must go now, darling. Are you quite sure that you don't want to come along with me?"

She smiled then and said, "No, love. You get on with your job. I'll be all right."

"Do talk to the doctor. I'm sure she'll be able to help you."

"I'll tell Dr. Corbett if I feel I need to."

"And tomorrow I'm free after lunch and we'll go off for the rest of the day. Down to Brighton if it's fine. And a theatre or a concert in the evening. Get you out of this house. It's enough to drive anyone into a nervous breakdown, living in this bloody morgue."

She nodded and smiled and kissed him goodbye but said no more.

It was not until some time later, when James was sitting in the car cursing at the heavy traffic, that he was struck by a very surprising thought. Not once, not in all those hours since he had come back to find Mary looking so strange, had either of them mentioned the Goff Papers. In fact, he did not think he had even thought about them during all that time, which was still more amazing.

CHAPTER 12

Mary remained at the front gate for several minutes after she had seen James's car turn the corner into the main road. He was driving into Central London and she was going to spend all day in a house in the suburbs, but it felt as if it were the other way about—that James was the static one, firmly enmeshed in the web of ordinary everyday life, while she herself had drifted out of it and was going on a journey, a long and dark and dangerous journey whose end she could not imagine. There was no way in which she could take a companion, for it was a journey of the mind, and nobody else knew that she was going, not even James.

For a moment or two she had been almost tempted not to go into that unknown darkness alone, but to cling blindly to him, hoping against all reasonable hope that he would succeed in pulling her back into the network of normal life. Perhaps he might have done so if he had been a different sort of character, but she knew his weakness only too well.

The man or woman who could rescue her now must have superhuman patience and strength, must give her an infinity of devotion and care; for in the world of everyday life she had become as helpless as a baby. It was only in the darkness of the mind that she had any strength or power of will.

But there was no way to explain this to James, and even if there had been, he could not have helped her any more than he had helped her already. He had realized that she had had a devastating shock that had cut away the shaky little foundation on which her life was built; and he had brought her greater love and tenderness than she had ever known. He had even understood, in a way, that she was looking into the darkness and could turn her eyes in no other direction. He had actually used the words "nervous breakdown," but he had no conception of what it really meant.

He had brought her much comfort, but it could not last. It was as if, at the outset of her dark journey, he had handed her a bouquet of flowers. Their colour and scent were strong and true, but they were doomed to fade, and their radiance become a memory. But it was better than nothing; it was better than if it had never existed at all.

"Goodbye, dear James," she murmured to herself when at last she returned to the house. "Think of me sometimes."

She was glad that their parting had been a loving one, for she knew that she was never going to see him again. By the time he had run through all his little busy-nesses—which to Mary's eye looked now as pointless as the scurryings of an insect on the floor—she herself would be well away. When her journey would start and what form it would take was not yet clear to her, but she knew that if she set about her preparations, it would all become plain and at every stage she would know exactly what to do.

The silence of the house enfolded her as she closed the front door. Now that she was going to leave it she understood for the first time how intolerable it was. Poor James. How he must have hated coming here. But soon he need come no more.

In the hall she paused. Normally she would have washed up and put the kitchen in order before proceeding to all the other insect-scurryings of her own meaninglessly busy little day. But there was hardly any washing up to do. Hector had an electric kettle and a tea-tray upstairs, and she might as well do the whole lot together later on.

There was, however, something else that she knew she must do straight away, before the doctor and the day-nurse arrived and she was caught up in the need to pretend that she was still a part of the everyday world.

She turned into the sitting-room and went straight to her desk on which stood the two photographs. The larger one—that of G. E. Goff—she merely glanced at before picking it up and laying it face-downwards in a drawer. He could wait a little. He would have to be dealt with before she made her own departure, but he would not run away, and she had plenty of time to decide what to do with him.

The smaller photograph occupied her for rather longer. A piece of paper in a cheap old cardboard frame. A little bit of rubbish. How very strange that it could have mattered so much. It looked just the same. But then a pearl would not change its outward appearance when one learned that it was made of paste. The change was in the mind of the viewer, and the Mary Morrison who had handled the little picture with such loving care was already dead; had died last night. The task of today's Mary was to tidy up after the deceased, and, when this had been accomplished, to join the other Mary.

She would start with this little picture. It was the most important part of her task, although by no means the hardest. Dealing with G. E. Goff would probably be the most difficult of all, because it involved other people, but what she must do would become plain to her when the time came. All of it was already written in the black book of fate, and she must turn the pages one by one.

A pasteboard frame. No metal about it. No need to remove it from the picture. The whole thing would burn.

But not in the house. Doctors and nurses, tiresome and irrelevant figures though they were, had nonetheless the power to interfere with her destiny and must therefore be avoided.

The garden would be best. Two days ago, when she was still part of the everyday world, Mary had made a bonfire to burn some of the dead leaves. The grass was damp today, and the leaves and twigs had ceased to smoulder, but there were a tin of paraffin in the garden shed, and some dry bits of wood and some old newspapers.

She quite enjoyed building up the funeral pyre for the little photograph. It seemed that this Mary, who had travelled far away from all earthly joys and pains, could still feel satisfaction at the sight of the leaping flames. It did not take very long for the photograph to burn, and she was sorry when it was over. Perhaps she could make greater fires later on; vast, splendid, all-consuming flames that would burn away the darkness.

All-healing flames. Their magic stayed with her, far eclipsing the little radiance of James's parting gift of loving concern.

She took a garden fork and prodded at the embers of the bonfire. Nothing was left of the photograph but ashes. So that task was done, but the fire had been so good that she must certainly make some more.

Back in the house, Hector Greenaway had meanwhile opened the front door to Dr. Corbett.

"How is our patient?" she asked.

"Doing fine, Doctor. Had a little read of a book last night and then slept right through, sweet as a new-born babe."

"That's good," she said. "I'll just take a look at him."

But at the bottom of the stairs she paused. "Where is Miss Morrison? Perhaps I ought to speak to her first."

"I don't know," replied Hector. "I haven't seen her this morning."

"Doesn't she come in to see her stepfather?"

"Not her. She don't care if he lives or dies, if you ask me, Doctor."

"What do you mean by that?" The plump face lost its cheerful look. "Is there something wrong with Miss Morrison? It's most unusual for her not to come to the door."

"Maybe she's gone off with the young man. I heard the car go."

"Mr. Greenaway," said the doctor severely, "I have great respect for the manner in which you are caring for your patient, and I am very pleased with his progress. But he is not my only concern in this household. I am interested in the welfare of his stepdaughter, and I should be grateful if you would kindly stop dropping hints and tell me straight out whether you think there is any cause for anxiety about her."

Hector, looking suitably subdued, glanced upstairs and then indicated the open door of the sitting-room. Dr. Corbett walked in and sat down. "Now," she said.

Hector remained standing. "I think she's out to do the old man a mischief," he said. "I reckon she's going a bit off her nut."

"Mary Morrison! Nonsense."

Hector shrugged and said no more.

"Of course she has been under considerable strain for a long time," went on Joan Corbett more calmly. "But now that she is going to marry young Mr. Goff, she has every reason to be happy and hopeful. They will have to make some provision for the old man to be looked after, of course, and there may be some difficulty about that." She paused. "Now, please tell me, Mr. Greenaway, and I don't want speculation, I want facts, what has happened to make you believe that Miss Morrison might want to 'do the old man a mischief,' as you put it."

"Because they had a quarrel last night—no, I can't rightly call it a quarrel, but he was scared of her, I could tell that; for although he sent me out of the room, I knew he wanted me to stay near so I could go to his help if need be. So I stayed right by the door and I put my ear to the keyhole and heard a little. Not much, but a little."

"Go on," said Dr. Corbett grimly.

"I heard her say, 'Forgive me.' It was something she'd said to him, and she was sorry for it. And I've known all along that that heart attack didn't come out of the blue," continued Hector excitedly, "and I told you, didn't I, Doctor?—that she'd been and said or done something that made the old man hopping mad, so mad that he nearly copped it."

"We know all about that. She told me herself. She asked him what he wanted done with his papers when he died, and he took it very badly and she felt guilty. Poor girl," continued Dr. Corbett gently. "It must have been preying on her mind very much."

"Well, he ain't forgiven her," said Hector. "He said something about her dad and her mum—sordid something or other was what I heard, and something about a fight in self-defence, and then I heard the bell and I came in right away, thinking she'd gone for him, but the old man was all right."

"What about Miss Morrison?"

"She was—sort of collapsed like. Never seen her like that before." Hector shook his head, looking rather bewildered.

"Good heavens!" cried Dr. Corbett. "Didn't you help her, man?"

"Course I helped her. Treated her for shock. Weak sweet tea and hot-water bottles and blankets and made sure she got into bed and left her some Mogadon tablets to take. Course I helped her."

"But she never said what was troubling her?"

"She didn't say nothing. But the young'un comes in soon after, and I don't reckon he was sleeping in the guest-room."

"You mean Mr. Goff's grandson?"

"That's right. I said to him, 'It's all yours, mate; I've got my own patient to look after.' "

"And this morning?" asked Dr. Corbett after a short pause.

"I've seen nobody. Heard the car go, though. About twenty minutes ago maybe."

The doctor stood up. "We must find her at once. Didn't it occur to you, Mr. Greenaway, that a shock strong enough to send Miss Morrison into the condition you describe is not to be recovered from in a matter of a few hours?"

"She's all right," muttered Hector. "She had the young'un to look after her."

"Yes, thank goodness, but I am nevertheless very concerned about Miss Morrison, and I cannot imagine why you think your patient might be in any danger from her. From what you have told me, it sounds the other way round—as if he has said something that might well have put her at risk of 'doing a mischief' to herself."

Hector looked puzzled again. "I dunno," he said at last. "It's just a feeling I got."

"Then try to forget it."

Joan Corbett walked briskly along the passage, closely followed by Hector. In the kitchen she said, "At least somebody seems to have had some breakfast."

"There she is!" cried Hector. He was standing by the sink, looking out of the window. "There she is. Right as rain. Putting the leaves on the bonfire."

Together they stood at the kitchen window and watched the tall slender figure, dressed in brown trousers and a scarlet sweater, moving to and fro pushing at the garden rubbish, very intent on her task.

"She certainly seems all right," said Dr. Corbett. "Is she usually out gardening as early as this?"

"I wouldn't know," was the reply. "I'm usually gone myself by this time."

"Oh, Mr. Greenaway, I am so sorry!" cried the doctor, turning away from the window and facing him. "I ought to have asked you straight away. Are you feeling very tired, or could you possibly stay on until tea-time? Mrs. Lowder can't manage this morning, but she can come at five o'clock and do the night duty as well. I thought I would ask you before calling the agency for another nurse. It's so much better to keep to the familiar faces, but I know it's a lot to ask of you."

"I don't mind," said Hector. "I've nothing else to do."

"Thank you very much indeed," said the doctor. "I'll just come up and have a look at our patient and then I must have a word with Miss Morrison and then I'll have to run or I'll be late for surgery. How time does fly."

She puffed her way upstairs and Hector followed her, still looking puzzled. This was the first time in a long association with Dr. Joan Corbett that she and he had not seen eye to eye. Of course he was sorry for Mary Morrison in a way, but it was her own fault. She ought to have had the sense to stand up to the old man. That was the way to handle him, and Hector himself was very proud of the way he managed this famous old man.

If she'd handled him right she could have had all those documents that they made such a fuss about, and the house and all the money too, and the young'un as well. If only she'd consulted him, Hector Greenaway; he could have told her how to set about it. But she always had been stand-offish, and that he could not abide. And now she had gone and offended the old man and he would never forgive her. And she, like many another weak and cornered creature, could turn dangerous in her desperation.

Hector felt this very strongly, but he could not explain why. Maybe it came from his years of experience in mental hospitals. He knew instinctively when somebody was going to break out into violence, and he had that feeling now. If the doctor wouldn't or couldn't understand, then he'd just have to keep a watch on the girl himself. He wasn't as young as he'd once been, and he'd been rather looking forward to going home and cooking himself some eggs and bacon and having a nice quiet read of the paper, but he'd get through the hours somehow and make sure nobody came to any harm, and if anything happened after he'd left the house, then nobody could say that it was his fault, because he'd have done his best.

CHAPTER 13

Mary had sensed that she was being watched, and knew that she must be very careful when other people were around. If she aroused suspicion, then she might not be able to fulfil her destiny. So when the photograph had burned away, she went to and fro with a garden fork, innocently and usefully occupied in disposing of the fallen leaves and the shrivelled prunings from the rose-bushes.

When Dr. Corbett came out to look for her, Mary was sweeping the path at the side of the house. She would much rather not have talked to the doctor at all, but since there was no avoiding it, it was easier here outdoors, where she could grip the broom to steady the trembling of her hands, and move about a bit, and turn her head aside at the flight of a bird, for her other self had been fond of the little garden birds, and it would be a good cover-up for her present intentions; for people who can chat about where the robin has been nesting this year are not people who have their minds full of images of the darkness of death and the splendour of leaping flames.

So runs the worldly wisdom, thought Mary. "He was always such an easygoing man; she always seemed such a well-balanced girl." Typical comments of the stupid everyday world when some tortured spirit had snatched at a knife to stab his torturer or some present-day Ophelia found some quicker oblivion than a river death. And they would say the same of her when she had ended her own journey. Mary Morrison, always so competent and self-controlled.

And then, because human nature cannot stand an unsolved mystery, they would try to find reasons for it. Of course there was always something odd and unnatural about her, they would say; of course one doesn't know what her natural father was like—bad blood there, maybe. Should she save them the trouble of searching for their tidy explanations, those silly scholars who believed that collecting little bits of paper would show them the way into other people's lives and minds? Perhaps, if she had time, she would write it all down. Except that they would misunderstand that, too, for words on paper had no power to convey the blazing darkness of the human mind.

The old man himself understood that well. They all admired his words on paper because he arranged them so much better than they could themselves, but he knew very well that truth could never come out that way. She and the old man—they knew each other without any juggling with words. He had destroyed her because she had destroyed him; but the shell of each survived, the hard part that did not so easily burn, and she must find a means to sweep these remnants away.

The broom scraped along the gravel path.

"Hullo, Mary," said Joan Corbett. "You're out gardening early today."

"There's a lot to do," she replied, "with the leaves falling so fast."

"Yes, indeed," said the doctor, "and I'm glad to see you getting some fresh air."

I can't think what Hector Greenaway can be talking about, she added to herself. There's nothing wrong with the girl, except that she doesn't look as happy as she did yesterday when James Goff was here; but then she has got a lot of problems to face. They both have. The old man is not going to make it easy for them, and Mary has such a conscience about him. And he must have upset her badly, telling her some horrible story about her natural father. Old people can be very vicious, particularly the clever ones.

"Yes, I like being out," agreed Mary.

If I could get her to talk about it, thought Dr. Corbett, she wouldn't feel so bad. But I'm late for surgery already and I can't get back here again until this evening . . . and Mr. Greenaway will keep an eye on her, and in any case she'll have told James all about it, and who better to help her than the man she's going to marry and who knows all the family situation very well?

"I suppose Mr. Goff—James—is in college today," she said.

"That's right," replied Mary. "He'll be back here this evening."

"So you'll have company," said Dr. Corbett, and Mary could almost hear the little click of relief with which the doctor transferred her sense of responsibility for Mary over to James. "You ought to get right away from the house for a while," she added. "It would do you good."

"James was talking of driving down to Brighton," said Mary.

The doctor's smile became even brighter. How easy it is to deceive them, thought Mary; it's child's play. How gladly they all catch at the happy lie that all is well. But this thought was followed by one that revealed a little flaw in her shield of contempt. James, last night, had not snatched at the lie. Of all people it had been the spoilt, selfish James who had refused to believe that all was well.

The remembrance brought a temporary weakness. If James had been there at that moment, acting as he had acted last night, she might have been in danger of diversion from her purpose. For he would certainly not go along with her all the way. He wished the old man dead, that was true, and together they could accomplish it more easily than she could alone. But at that point their common interest stopped, for James would like G. E. Goff the writer to live on for ever, reflecting his light upon his grandson; while the Mary of today, who had been contained in but concealed by the Mary of yesterday and all the preceding days, wanted above all things to extinguish that light.

Books. Millions of them throughout the world, translated into many languages, printed in every sort of edition. These she could not touch. But there were some things that lay within her power, and James would be a hindrance here, and not a help.

The weakness passed. Mary accompanied the doctor to her car, talking about James's work.

"Take it easy today," said Joan Corbett as they parted. "And try not to worry about your stepfather. Mr. Greenaway will look after him till five o'clock and Nurse Lowder will relieve him then, so there is no need for you to do anything at all."

Dr. Corbett paused. She still felt that she ought to refer to the incident about which Hector had told her, since it did not look as if Mary was going to mention it herself, but she did not want the girl to know that they had been talking about her, and could see no way to approach the subject tactfully. Perhaps it was best to leave it alone. After all, Mary seemed to be quite recovered, and no doubt she had told James about it, and he would be back this evening.

"Is Mrs. Lowder coming at five?" asked Mary. This was a bonus indeed. Hector Greenaway was her greatest obstacle.

"She'll stay on through the night," was the reply. "I don't think there will be very much for her to do. And tomorrow we must talk about making some other arrangements. I can't help feeling that a period in a nursing home would be the best thing, because eventually, my dear, you are going to have to relieve yourself of the care of him, and this is a good moment to make the break. I am sure we shall find James Goff of great help here. Now I really must fly. Goodbye, Mary. Have a good day. Just you do exactly what you want to for a change."

"Yes," said Mary quietly, "I am going to do exactly what I want to. Goodbye, Dr. Corbett, and thank you very much for all your help."

The doctor paused with her hand on the door of her car. There was a sort of solemn finality in the girl's speech that seemed out of place in the circumstances. Could the little nurse be right after all? Could Mary really be contemplating suicide? That she had a tendency to depression the doctor had always known; but then living with G. E. Goff was enough to depress anybody. Mary's mother had, of course, carried the chief burden of it, and in Dr. Corbett's opinion, Christina's death from pneumonia at the age of fifty-six was partly due to the fact that the poor woman had had no resistance to illness at all, no fight left in her. And during the last few years it had rather looked as if Mary might be going the same way, but now she had James and a happy future to look forward to, and that, thought Dr. Corbett as she drove off down the road, very conscious of the fact that she was going to be very late for surgery, must be enough to heal any wound that her stepfather's acid tongue had inflicted.

So the doctor, too, was soon swept back into the everyday world, and in the house in Chestnut Close there remained only the sick old man and his elderly nurse and Mary herself.

At half past ten in the morning Richard telephoned Paula and they arranged to spend the following Sunday together.

"But this time you must come to me for a meal," she said. "I'm going to undertake a labour of Hercules. I'm going to tidy up the flat."

Richard was suitably impressed. Then he said, "Have you seen James at all this morning?"

"No, but he must be around somewhere. I'm going over to the common room in a minute or two and I'll probably see him there."

"I'm wondering whether Mary has told him about the Goff Papers coming to me. Could you possibly find out?"

"I'm wondering too," said Paula. "It oughtn't to be too difficult to find out. If James is in a bad mood, nobody is allowed to ignore it."

"Paula."

"Richard?"

"I do not seem to be feeling as joyful as I had expected. There's something rather painful about being the winner in this case. But it doesn't make any difference to my gratitude to you."

"I know," sighed Paula. "Conscience. I've got it badly too. Not so much towards James."

"But towards Mary. I can't stop thinking about her. I should very much like to know how she is, but I don't think a call from me would be welcome at the moment."

"So you'd like me to ask James about her. I was going to do that in any case."

"Bless you," said Richard. "I realize that you are in a somewhat embarrassing situation as regards James Goff."

Paula laughed. "I am indeed. But I put myself into it, so must not complain. When can I call you back?"

"I'm working at home all afternoon, so any time up till six will do. But, Paula—"

"Yes?"

"Take care of yourself."

"Are you afraid that I am going to be the object of James's fury and revenge?"

"Well, you did say yourself that James . . ." began Richard, and then paused for a moment. "I don't know why I feel so uneasy," he went on. "The old man is receiving all possible medical care, and as we agreed last night, there is now no possible motive for—"

He broke off again. "Sorry to be so incoherent," he said at last. "Please tell me what I am talking about, Paula."

"I think you're talking about Mary Morrison, and that she seems destined to be a loser, since she can't rely on James without the Goff Papers."

"She's got absolutely nobody to turn to for help," said Richard, "and I'm the last person to be of any use to her now."

"I've changed my mind," said Paula decisively. "I'm not going to waste time trying to talk to James here at college. He'll probably refuse to speak to me, and in any case you can't have any conversation here without constant interruptions. There's a couple of students whom I have to see this morning, and after that I'm free till our Department party at six o'clock. That gives me plenty of time to go and inspect the Goff household for myself. If it's the same nurse there as it was yesterday, I'll have no trouble getting in. And if it's Mary herself—well, if I were in her position, I'd be bursting with curiosity about James's ex-girl friend, and I'm sure all females are alike in this respect. There you are, Richard. You shall have a firsthand report on Chestnut Close."

"Paula, you are incomparable."

"No credit to me, pal. I'm bursting with curiosity myself."

At the same time as their telephone conversation was

taking place, James in a room farther along the corridor was asking Hector Greenaway if he would call Mary to the phone. When she spoke at last he did not, as he had intended, ask her how she was and tell her how much he was thinking about her, but said instead, "Why is that wretched little man still there? I thought he was only on night duty."

"Mrs. Lowder can't come till five," was the reply.

"Oh, I see. Well, I suppose at least he can keep Grandpa quiet and you don't need to be bothered at all," said James.

"No, I don't need to be bothered at all," agreed Mary.

"Are you all right, love? You don't sound very bright. You're not still worrying about—"

"I'm perfectly all right. I've been gardening. That's why Hector answered the phone."

"And what are you going to do now?"

"Go shopping. Come home and make some lunch. Then do a bit of typing. Rest a little if I can."

"That's good. You could do with some rest. As long as you're all right."

James was rather at a loss. Something seemed to have gone wrong with the conversation. She sounded perfectly calm, but very remote, and it was not just because they were on a bad line. He would have liked to try once more to ask if she was fully recovered from last night, but it was obvious that she didn't want to talk about it. And he would also have liked to ask about the Goff Papers, because now that last night's crisis was over, they were once more in the forefront of his mind. But this was not the moment to talk about them either. Telephoning was never very satisfactory on an occasion like this. It would have been so much easier if they could have been together today. There was a knock on the door of his room. "Damn," said

James into the telephone, "there's a boy come for his tutorial. Goodbye, darling, I'll ring again. Take care."

Mary put down the receiver and walked out of the sitting-room into the hall. Hector was standing at the foot of the stairs. "What would you like for your lunch?" she asked. "I'm going shopping now."

She looked and sounded just the same as before the events of the last few days. Quiet and calm, polite but unwilling to chat. Hector was puzzled. It was as if her last night's collapse had never been. And yet he still had this feeling about her; it was like a sort of sixth sense in him, and up till now this instinct of his had never failed him.

"Don't you go bothering about any lunch for me, Miss Morrison," he said.

"But you must have something to eat. You didn't expect to be staying here all day and you haven't brought any sandwiches."

"I tell you what I'll do," said Hector confidentially. "While you're out shopping, I'll nip down to the kitchen and make an omelette for myself and the old 'un. If you don't mind me taking the liberty of helping myself."

"All right. If that's what you want."

It was said with complete indifference. Maybe she thinks I'm suspicious of any food she prepares for the old man, thought Hector, but at least she can't be afraid of my snooping around, or she'd have reacted differently. In fact, she wouldn't have left the house at all.

But the opportunity of having the free run of the house was too good to miss. After he and his patient had had a meal, Hector left the old man dozing, and wandered around for a while. He had already taken a mental inventory of the main rooms on those rare occasions when Mary had been out for the evening, and his memory was excellent. Two things only appeared to him to be not as usual.

The first was that the photographs that normally stood on top of the bureau in the sitting-room were not there; and the second was more an impression than a certainty. It seemed to him that the piles of black-covered notebooks that lay on the shelf by the door in the study were not as high as they had been the last time he came into the room.

Whether there was any significance in either or both of these changes he could not tell, but he stored the facts in his memory. It would have been interesting to go into Mary Morrison's bedroom, but he hesitated to do so, because he could think of no excuse at all for being there and it would put him in the wrong if he was caught.

Besides, the old man had woken up and was getting restless. His bell rang when Hector was in the study, taking out of a drawer a folder that looked as if it might contain some interesting letters, and made him start guiltily.

"What are you doing?" grumbled G. E. Goff. "Where have you been?"

"Washing up and making us a cup of tea," replied the nurse. "Won't be a minute."

"I don't want any tea. I want to get up."

"Now, now, chief. Doctor says you can sit up a bit tomorrow if you keep on as well as you are. Tomorrow. Not till then."

"Doctor's a fool. I want to look at my study. I don't trust them."

"What do you want to look at in the study?" said Hector soothingly. "You tell me what you want and I'll go and fetch it. You can trust me, can't you?"

The reply was a grunt which Hector took as assent.

"D'you want me to fetch you another book to read? Or some of them old papers?"

"I want the file of reviews of *Last Judgement*," said

G. E. Goff firmly. "If you can't find it you will have to ask Mary. But don't let her come near me. I can't do with all this weeping and wailing. Silly girl. Thought she'd learned more sense by now. Get her to give it to you if you can't find it, and you bring me the file, and then I want you to lock the study door and put the key under my pillow. Don't trust them. Don't trust them at all."

"Okay, chief, I won't be long," said Hector. "But don't you try any funny business when I'm gone. We don't want any more of these heart attacks, do we? Might not pull out of it quite so quickly the next time."

It didn't take him long to find the right box file, but there was no key in the study door, and it was Hector's belief that Mary Morrison had given the keys to James Goff. Following his normal policy of humouring the patient whenever possible, he looked around for a similar type of key, and decided that the one in the bathroom door would do. G. E. Goff accepted it without question and demanded that the contents of the box file should be laid out on the bed table for his inspection. This proved to be a laborious procedure, since the table was rather too high for the old man to pore over the papers in comfort, and the awkwardness of his fingers caused him to be constantly losing items that he wanted.

Among Hector Greenaway's many excellent qualities as a nurse was an almost inexhaustible store of patience, but today he was becoming tired from the long hours on duty and he was also not used to the sort of demands now being made on him. After struggling for some time to find the bits of paper that G. E. Goff seemed to want, Hector found his patience wearing rather thin, and he also began to have a feeling of sympathy for Mary, who must have spent many hours in just this sort of situation. If she did indeed feel murderous towards the old man, it was hardly to be wondered at.

At last everything was arranged to the patient's satisfaction, and Hector leaned back in his armchair with a sigh of relief, and silence reigned in the house once more.

CHAPTER 14

Mary bought a few cans of food at random so that when she returned to the house it would look as if she really had been doing some household shopping, and then went to the garden department of the big store in the main street and looked thoughtfully at the displays of artificial flowers and dried flowers.

The honesty, with its abundance of thin, flat seed pods, would probably be best; the pampas grass perhaps not as good; but pink and purple statice would add colour to the white honesty, and perhaps some of the smaller grasses. Even if nobody else ever saw the arrangement, it had still got to look right. The vital thing about her day's preparations was that every single thing she said and did must appear to fit in perfectly with the vision of those who were still living in that strange, unreal, world of everyday that she had once inhabited herself.

"How about some beech leaves?" suggested the saleswoman. "Or do you have enough of your own?"

Mary was a regular customer and well liked by the staff. She always knew what she wanted and she bought generously.

"No, that's enough, thanks," she said, "but I'd like to see your new rose catalogue when it's available."

The saleswoman promised to forward a copy, and also of anything else that might interest her. "I heard that Mr. Goff was ill," she added. "I hope he's better now."

"Much better, thank you."

The whole conversation was a perfect example of the little flow of everyday life. It was so easy; it only required a little thought at the right moments.

But when she got back to Chestnut Close, Mary found that her confident balancing of the two worlds, the dark one and the world of the commonplace, was somewhat shaken by the sight of somebody standing on the front doorstep, a fair-haired young woman wearing a blue raincoat. Mary stared at her mistrustfully, uncertain and confused, as if she were acting in a play and had momentarily forgotten her lines.

"Excuse me," said the newcomer. "It's Mary Morrison, isn't it? I'm Paula Glenning. I saw you yesterday after I'd been calling here with Richard, who is a friend of mine, and I wanted him to introduce us, but he hurried me away. And I know James too. I teach in the same Department. I expect he told you."

Mary made no reply. She was very laden with her shopping bag and the big bunch of dried flowers and was having difficulty in finding her front-door key.

"Shall I take the flowers?" suggested Paula.

"Thank you. That would be a help."

The little exchange had given Mary her cue. By the time they were inside the house and she had retrieved the flowers, the mechanism for dealing with all the little irrelevancies around her was once more functioning.

"If you'll excuse me," she said, "I'll put these into a vase right away because they so easily become damaged if you don't keep them upright. I'll be with you in a moment if you'd like to take a seat. Or would you like to come along to the kitchen and join me in a cup of coffee?"

"Thanks," said Paula, choosing the latter alternative.

Passion hidden by primness, she said to herself; that's how Richard described her. Was she angry at this intrusion? Jealous? Resentful? Suspicious? It was quite impossible to tell what she was feeling. Paula had seldom felt quite so much at a loss, but she had come out here for Richard's sake, because he was worrying so much about Mary, and she was determined to plod on.

"How is Mr. Goff?" she asked.

"Much better, thanks," replied Mary, measuring coffee into the pot.

Behind her back Paula made a grimace. This was an impossible situation she had got herself into. There seemed nothing to be done except make a few polite remarks, drink a cup of coffee, and go away, having achieved nothing except that she could tell Richard that Mary was certainly not prostrate with despair. But even if she were feeling like that, thought Paula, I don't believe she would show it.

"I'm afraid you must think it rather odd, my coming to see you today," she said.

"You are very welcome," replied Mary formally, "although I can't help wondering which one of them has asked you to come—Richard or James."

"Oh my God, it must look absolutely awful!" cried Paula in a much more natural tone of voice. "You must be sick to death of people pestering you about the Goff Papers, but of course it's all settled now, with Mr. Goff bequeathing them to Richard. He told me about it yesterday after we left here, and I was actually with him when he phoned you, and although he's so pleased about it, he's feeling guilty because it was a rather thoughtless way to let you know if you didn't know already, and he more or less sent me here today to apologize."

"He need not have worried," said Mary, "and neither need you. There's nothing to apologize for. It's all perfectly straightforward."

"Then you don't mind so very much?"

"Why should I mind?" Mary looked straight at Paula as

she said this. She was frowning slightly and seemed genuinely puzzled by the question.

Paula felt more curtained off than ever, but she struggled gamely on. "Richard thought that you would want James to have the papers, and that you'd be disappointed."

"If it's worrying him so much," said Mary in the same unemotional tones, "he can always refuse the bequest."

It was at this point that Paula became certain that Mary was silently laughing at her, and it was a very disagreeable feeling. To be openly abused for her interference would have been far more tolerable. But there was no denying that Mary had cause for resentment, and if this was her way of showing it, there was nothing more to be done. Richard would be distressed, but less so than if he thought Mary was feeling helplessly hurt, for it is easier to bear another's anger than one's own sense of guilt.

Paula finished her coffee and stood up. "I'm sorry," she said. "I wish we could have met in different circumstances. But since we are backing different horses and they can't both of them win, there's no way that we could become friends, as I should have liked."

Mary made no response. The sense of smouldering laughter behind the grave dark eyes was becoming harder and harder to endure.

"Oh, I nearly forgot," said Paula when they were in the front hall. "Could I ask you a small favour? Could I please have a word with Nurse Lowder?"

"She's not here," replied Mary. "The male nurse is still on duty."

"Then could I have her address? Richard promised her a ticket for one of the *Watch Your Words* recordings, but doesn't know where to send it."

"I don't know where she lives," replied Mary. "Dr. Corbett sent her. But we can phone the surgery and find out."

She led the way into the sitting-room and picked up the telephone that stood on one of the low tables. Paula glanced around her. Everything looked the same as yesterday except that the photographs were gone from the top of the bureau, and lying on the blotter was a little pile of unopened mail.

"I'll have to do some office work this afternoon," said Mary as she dialled. "The cleaning woman is away, so it's been household chores this morning."

Paula could find nothing to say.

"No, I don't want to speak to the doctor," Mary was saying into the phone. "It's only to ask if you have Mrs. Jane Lowder's address. She's coming here to do night duty this evening, and I've got rather an urgent message for her."

A minute later Paula was copying an address and a telephone number into her pocket diary. "Thanks for taking the trouble," she said.

"You're very welcome," replied Mary.

For the first time in the whole encounter there was a hint of warmth and goodwill in her voice. But why should she be thawing out, wondered Paula, over a trivial business of getting the nurse's address and telephone number? The only explanation she could think of was that Mary was looking forward to getting rid of her unwelcome visitor.

But apparently the goodwill was to be carried a little further.

"Would you like to see the great man's study?" said Mary. "Since you're teaching literature, it would probably interest you."

"Thank you," said Paula, taken aback. "Yes, I would."

She followed Mary upstairs like a privileged visitor accompanying the curator of a museum to view treasures not normally on show. Mary opened a cream-painted door and stood aside. "All the novels were written in this room," she said in the voice of an official guide.

Paula took a step into the room. The impression was of darkness, although the bay window was large and the crimson curtains were drawn back. There were two walls lined with books from floor to ceiling, with shelves, cupboards, and filing cabinets against the rest of the wall space. A big leather-topped desk; an armchair and small table; several upright chairs, a few other small items of furniture. No space on the walls for pictures; no china, no ornaments of any kind, no brightness, no frivolity, no evidence of any human weakness. A museum piece. A dark, dead room. A horrible place.

And yet, for millions of readers and listeners and viewers all over the world, now and for years to come, life had been created in this room. It ought to be shining and triumphant. Instead, it was stifling.

"This is not the original desk," continued Mary in her dutiful and impersonal voice, "but was bought only ten years ago. Previous to that . . ."

When she paused for a moment, Paula tried to think of something appropriate to say, something expressive of interest and reverence that one ought to feel when visiting the homes of the great. But nothing came into her mind except her intense dislike of the room. Even the book shelves, which anywhere else would have drawn her like a magnet, were in this place repulsive to her, and she moved away from them after the merest glance at a couple of titles, and drew closer to Mary, who was still standing by the desk.

Paula looked at her keenly, wondering what she really felt about her famous stepfather. Perhaps something of her sympathetic interest communicated itself, for Mary dropped her official manner, and for the first time during the visit really looked straight at Paula.

"You find it gloomy here," she said, more as a statement than as a question. "So do I. I always have done. When I was a young child I used to think that this room was the Valley of the Shadow . . . like in the psalm."

"I can quite understand that," said Paula in quiet but heartfelt tones.

She waited for further confidences, but none came. Mary seemed to have withdrawn into her own thoughts and Paula hesitated to disturb her. Perhaps she could just creep away unnoticed. The silent oppressiveness of the room was becoming intolerable and she felt scarcely able to breathe. At last, just when Paula was beginning to fear that she might lose control of herself and go into the sort of claustrophobic panic that occasionally attacked her, Mary moved towards the door, smiled faintly, and said, "I'll put the flowers in here—that'll cheer it up a little," and led the way downstairs.

Paula followed, still very much in the grip of the sensations that G. E. Goff's study had aroused in her, but also full of a compassion for Mary that insisted on being expressed.

"I wish I could be of some help to you," she said as they once again stood together on the front doorstep. "You have heavy responsibilities to bear. I wish you would look on me as a friend."

Mary made no reply, but Paula sensed that she was not entirely hostile, and this brought the courage to go on.

"It's none of my business," she said, "and you've every right to resent my interference, but I must say this, I really must. Do think very carefully before you marry James. It will mean that you'll never be free of G. E. Goff and all his works. Even if James doesn't inherit all that stuff upstairs, he'll never leave it alone. He'll be niggling away at it for ever. Oh, Mary, I do so wish you could get away from here and have a chance to find out what you really want from life. Please try. Please, please do try. Get away from literature and books. They're death to the living."

Impulsively she caught hold of the girl's hands. She was going farther than she had intended, but she could not stop herself. It was as if in that room upstairs she had had a glimpse of the forces of darkness and had to try, with all the strength of her own vitality and of her own vision of life and freedom, to fight against them.

"I used to think," she went on, "that human genius was a divine gift, that it had the right to make demands on ordinary folk like you and me, and that we ought to make allowances for it, perhaps even make sacrifices for it. But I don't think so any more."

She looked up at Mary's face. It was several inches above her own and was still without any marked expression. But at least she had not pulled her hands away, nor looked or spoken her displeasure or contempt.

"Here's my phone number and address," went on Paula. "If there's anything at all that I can do for you—if you ever want a refuge, or to talk to somebody who will make no demands on you, well, here I am. And if it's any comfort to you at all, don't forget that I do understand."

"Thank you." Mary's voice was very low. She was looking a little bewildered now.

Paula reached up and kissed her. "Don't forget," she said again.

She retrieved her shoulder-bag, which was slipping to the ground, walked hurriedly to the gate, glanced back to smile and to wave, and then walked slowly along the road under the chestnut trees, deep in thought.

Mary stood looking after her, as a few hours earlier she had stood watching James's car drive away.

"You understand," she muttered. "Why yes, I believe you do. How very strange. I didn't think anybody ever would. You see the problem very clearly—almost as clearly as I see it myself. But you don't see a solution. Oh no, even you haven't begun to guess at my solution."

She laughed aloud, then pressed both hands to her mouth to try to stop it, appalled by her sudden loss of control.

"It's you who've done this, Paula Glenning," she said. "You've weakened me, you've taken away my strength with your charming ways and your seductive sympathy. Damn you. Damn you!"

Had she been speaking out loud? She no longer knew. She shut the front door and ran round the side of the house and across the lawn to the garden shed, where she shut herself in and leaned against the trestle-table on which the pots with geranium cuttings stood. Damn you, damn you, shrieked her mind, while her fingers twisted together and her head moved violently from side to side.

It was the worst moment of the whole day. The talk with Dr. Corbett had been nothing like as bad as this. After a while she became calmer, but her mind continued to talk to Paula. So you understand, do you? But nobody knows what to do about it except me. And you are going to be just as surprised as everybody else when I do it.

This last thought made her laugh again, and this time there was no need to stifle it. Here in the garden shed she was out of sight and hearing of any other human being. She clung to the trestle-table and shook with laughter.

"Thank you, Paula Glenning," she said when at last it died away. "That did me good. And thank you too for showing me what to do about Nurse Lowder. I was wondering how I was going to get rid of her, but much the best thing will be if she never comes here at all, and now that I've got her phone number . . ."

There was only one major difficulty left: how to persuade Hector to leave before another nurse had arrived, but as the hours wore on, Mary felt sure that she would find a solution to this as well.

In the underground train Paula sat for some time with her eyes closed, exhausted and deeply distressed and feeling as if nothing was ever going to be the same again. It was as if she had seen too closely into other lives, had torn aside what ought to have remained hidden. What right had she to tell Mary Morrison what to do? How could she possibly know what a life lived under the shadow of G. E. Goff had been like? She herself had had her troubles and had made plenty of mistakes, but she had always known freedom of the spirit, had never had to struggle to achieve a sense of her own identity.

And yet at the time it had felt right to speak out. She had had an overpowering sense of oppression in that horrible dark, dead room, and had seen Mary as trapped and crushed by it, unable to free herself.

But did Mary really feel like that? After all, there had been that moment, before they went upstairs, when Paula had felt sure that Mary was silently laughing at her. And she had been calm and composed, even when recalling her childhood fear of G. E. Goff's study. It was Paula who had given way to her feelings. Was Mary such a helpless victim? Had she found her own way out?

Perhaps she had made up her mind to murder the old man. Perhaps she had already done so. There had been no sense of life in the house, no sign of any other living creature at all.

I'm imagining things, Paula told herself severely as she got out of the train at Russell Square Station and her legs started moving, without her telling them to, in the direction of Richard's flat; but there's one thing I'm quite sure about: If the old man is dead and the Goff Papers are left to Richard, then I can't give him any help with them. I don't even want to see the wretched things, and nothing on earth will ever induce me to go into that room again.

CHAPTER 15

Hector woke with a start out of a sleep much deeper than his usual catnap when on duty, and took several seconds to remember where he was. The first thing he noticed was that the room was very dark—only the dim lamp was burning. He glanced at his watch, saw that it was past four o'clock, and thought with very great relief that it was not much longer now before he would be able to go home.

He ought never to have agreed to do this extra stretch of duty. He was an old man now. It had been different in the hospital years. He'd been younger then, and although they'd always been overworked, there had been a lot of them in it together. He'd only taken on the G. E. Goff job to oblige Dr. Corbett, and yes, be honest, because the patient was famous and very old and it was likely there'd be something left to Hector when the death came. And up till now it had worked out very well, except that the girl had been so unfriendly, not the sort of person you could chat to at all, and it wasn't even as if she were his real daughter. Just an illegitimate nobody.

Hector got slowly up from his armchair and looked at the bed. The old man seemed to be asleep, his mouth was open and his head was at an awkward angle on the pillow. The table and the bedcover were strewn with newspaper cuttings, pages from old journals, sheets of typescript, crumpled-up old newspapers. Hector looked at them in dismay. I'm a nurse, he said to himself; not a bloody secretary.

The hours before they both went to sleep had been the most trying time that Hector had ever spent with this patient. G. E. Goff, with his body still very weak but his mind restored to all its former agitation and irritability, had been cursing Hector for not instantly finding whatever piece of paper that he wanted; had tried to dictate a letter to him, becoming even more furious when he was told that Hector couldn't write shorthand; demanded that Mary be sent for, and become quite unmanageable when told that she had gone out shopping.

Peace had only been restored when Hector had succeeded in giving him one of the sedative tablets that Dr. Corbett had prescribed for such emergencies, and Hector, worn out himself, had fallen asleep as well. Thus they had been when Mary took Paula upstairs.

Hector switched on the kettle and brewed strong tea. I hope he's dead, he muttered to himself as he sipped it; I've had enough. It's the last time I come to this house.

But he knew very well that the old man was not dead, and that any moment he would wake and the whole intolerable performance would start all over again. Mrs. Lowder will just have to cope with him, said Hector to himself, somewhat restored by his tea, and if she can't, she'll have to call that crazy girl. No wonder she's off her nut; I'd be the same way if I had this all the time. Another half hour to go.

The head on the pillow stirred and raised itself. Hector groaned inwardly.

"Now, chief," he said in a feeble imitation of his usual confident tones, "what's the drill? Bedpan? Cuppa tea?"

G. E. Goff struggled to sit up, glaring at the closed door. "There's somebody in the study," he said. "I told you to lock it."

"It is locked, chief, and there's nobody there."

"I don't believe it. They're trying to rob me. I'm going to see."

"Oh my God!" cried Hector. "Just you stay there," he added firmly, taking the old man by the shoulders and pushing him back against the pillow. "Don't move, or you'll have another heart attack. I'll go and see for myself. Won't be long. Be good now."

It was the sort of treatment that had always worked in the past, but either Hector was losing his touch or else the old man had become more difficult than ever. Senile dementia, thought the nurse as he walked to the door of the bedroom and shut it behind him; that's what we'll have next, and God help whoever has to look after him.

The study door was wide open. He saw Mary before she saw him. The curtains were drawn across the window, the centre light was on, and she was standing by the desk with her back to him. Spread over the desk was an assortment of dried leaves and flowers, and she was intent on her task of arranging them in a big wooden bowl that was normally used for fruit and salads. It was a pale, polished wood, and it suited the autumnal colours. Hector had to admit that she was making a good job of it. Careful, neat, but artistic. He always liked to see a job well done.

It was funny, though, that although she looked calmly intent on her task, he still had this feeling about her that he had mentioned to Dr. Corbett, as if somehow or other she was going to "break out" before long. Then he told himself that it was none of his business. He was doing his duty—far more than his fair share of duty, in fact—and they'd all have to look out for themselves. In any case, the way he felt about G. E. Goff at this moment, if Mary Morrison was really planning to smother or strangle him, then he, Hector Greenaway, so far from trying to stop her, would be more inclined to help her to accomplish it.

"That looks pretty, Miss Morrison," he said at last.

"Yes," she replied without looking up. "I thought it was time the bowl in Mr. Goff's room was removed, but I didn't want to disturb him while I was doing the new arrangement."

"Why don't you leave them in here," said Hector. "They'd cheer this old room up a bit."

"I may do that." Mary stood back to survey her work.

Hector came nearer. "How do you hold the stems in place?" The way things worked always interested him, and he had never had cause to inspect any flower-arranging at close quarters before. "Oh, I see. It's that spongy stuff I've seen in florists' shops."

"When it's for fresh flowers, you can soak it in water," explained Mary, "and it keeps them damp and fresh. But that's not necessary here. I may perhaps stuff some old paper round the stems later on, to fill up the bowl a bit."

"Plenty of old paper in here," said Hector, glancing round at the cupboards and the shelves and the filing cabinets, and laughing as he spoke.

Mary laughed too, and it sounded quite natural to him. "That's blasphemy," she said.

He was about to make some remark about the old man's books, some clever comment about the contrast between all that fame on the one hand, and the grumpy old nuisance next door on the other, when G. E. Goff's bell rang loudly. Very reluctantly Hector went to answer it. Just like the old blighter to go and ring now, he thought, when for the first time ever he was enjoying a really interesting conversation with Miss Morrison. By the time he got away again she'd have finished the job and might not be in the right mood for a chat.

"There's nobody in the study," he said to the old man. "I told you so. I've locked it up again and here's the key." Once more he slipped the key of the bathroom under the pillow.

But like a child who senses the growing impatience of those caring for it, G. E. Goff became more and more querulous and demanding; and the nurse, up till now so proud of his ability to manage him, became more and more frustrated and irritable. In the end he got his patient to swallow another tranquillizer, but that was the maximum dose for the day, and Dr. Corbett would not be too pleased. And as for Nurse Lowder, once the effect of the drug wore off and the patient started all this nonsense over again . . .

But that wasn't his worry, Hector told himself firmly. He'd done his duty, and more, and nobody could blame him for anything. The old man was quiet again at last, and with any luck would remain so for a couple of hours. Hector tidied up the papers scattered over the bedspread as best he could, made a note of the medicines that had been administered, and left it on top of the chest of drawers together with the bottles, collected his own belongings, and went downstairs. It was nearly time for him to be relieved of duty. Maybe Mrs. Lowder had arrived already.

But downstairs there was only Mary sitting at her desk typing. She looked up and smiled at him, a very bright and friendly smile. Hector blinked, more puzzled than ever. Maybe I'm wrong about her, he said to himself; maybe here's the exception that proves the rule.

"Hasn't Mrs. Lowder come?" he asked.

"Not yet," replied Mary. "I'm afraid she's going to be a little late. She phoned to say she was at her daughter's and is just leaving now."

This was based on the truth. In fact, when Mary telephoned Mrs. Lowder to tell her that there was no need for her to come in till eight o'clock, the nurse had replied that that was very convenient, because it meant that she could have her grandson with her for another couple of hours, which would suit the child's parents very well. It's so easy,

Mary had thought yet again, so long as you remember that people will always believe what they want to believe.

Hector looked disappointed. He also looked very tired. "How long is she likely to be?" he asked.

"Not very long, I expect," was Mary's reply. "But of course it rather depends on the traffic."

Don't suggest that he should go away now, she said to herself; let the suggestion come from him. It looked as if she might be in luck, and that he was going to leave the house in the normal way, which was a very big bonus indeed, because it would save her the trouble of getting him to swallow the knock-out dose that she had prepared for him. The friendly little chat upstairs had paved the way for them to have a drink together, and she knew he liked his whisky, and the spirit would disguise the taste of the drug; but she would much prefer him to be right away from the house instead of slumped on the floor in the garden shed, not to mention the difficulty of getting him there in the wheelbarrow. He was only a little fellow, and the garden was dark and not overlooked by any of the neighbouring houses, but nevertheless it was going to be awkward. On no account must she have him unconscious in the house.

"How is Mr. Goff?" she asked, looking at Hector with a sympathetic expression on her face.

He looked at this moment rather a sad little figure, this biggest and final obstacle to the fulfilment of her destiny, standing there in his dark-blue raincoat with his grey hair limp and his eyes narrow and strained from weariness; and holding in his left hand a bag labelled "Concorde" that he always used for carting around his folded-up working coat and his medical requirements; and his favourite brand of biscuits, and his newspaper, and his little hand-towel, and whatever else he might feel he would have a use for during his duty hours.

He was a tough little old man, but every single thing about him, at that moment, seemed to cry out his overwhelming longing to be home.

"He's sleeping," replied Hector to Mary's question. "He's been restless and I've given him the sedative the doctor prescribed. I've written it all down, what he's had. He'll sleep for the next couple of hours without giving any trouble."

"Then he won't need any attendance," said Mary.

"No. There'll be no need for anyone to sit with him."

"And Dr. Corbett will be coming in later this evening," said Mary. "I'm afraid you've had a long and tiring time of it today."

"Well, I was rather looking forward to going off duty now," said Hector, glancing at his watch.

"Well, then."

"D'you mean you really don't mind if I don't wait for Mrs. Lowder? There's nothing to be done for him at the moment, Miss Morrison. I should just leave him alone if I was you."

"I shall certainly leave him alone. I've got a great deal of typing to get on with. I haven't even finished the letters he dictated the day before yesterday."

"Marvellous, ain't it," said Hector, "the way his mind does keep turning over and over. You'd think it would want a rest by this time."

Mary smiled and nodded. "Thank you for all you've done. Dr. Corbett will be in touch with you. Don't worry about him. You go off and have a good rest yourself. I believe you could do with it."

"I could that, and that's a fact."

He seemed to hesitate for a moment and then made up his mind. Why should I bother? he asked himself; I've done more than anybody else would, more than anybody had any right to ask me to do. And after all, she's the mistress of this house, she's responsible for what happens here, not me. She seems fine now, but one never knows. . . . I still can't get rid of that feeling . . . but after all, I did tell Dr. Corbett and she just told me to forget it. So I'm going to forget it. I've had enough, I have.

In his mind's eye he could see his snug little living-room, with his armchair and his footstool and his new television. And his cat Blackie, who would be raging hungry by this time unless the woman next door had thought to feed her.

It was like a vision of Paradise.

"Well, if you really think it's all right, Miss Morrison . . ."

"You go and enjoy your well-earned rest," she said.

After Hector had gone she sat for a moment thinking of him with great goodwill, almost with affection. He had made it so easy for her, and she would far rather think of him as happy and comfortable in his own home than lying drugged and unconscious on the cold floor of the garden shed.

It was a good omen, Hector's going off so peacefully like that; it meant that everything was going to work out. She felt so sure of this that she even finished typing the letter. It was the vitriolic one, addressed to the young Richard Grieve, who as a university student had dared to judge *Last Judgement,* comparing it, not entirely in its favour, with an earlier G. E. Goff novel.

The typing eased her excitement. There was no great hurry now. Everything was ready, apart from one or two last-minute touches and the big question, posed by Hector's information that G. E. Goff was fast asleep: Should she do it straight away, or should she wake him up and tell him that he was going to die? It seemed a pity not to take advantage of the work started by the sedative, but on the other hand she had rather looked forward to telling him what was going to happen.

After a little reflection she decided on the first alternative. She was not cruel by nature and her task was to carry out a judgement, not to inflict torment. She had caused him distress, that was true, but she had genuinely repented and that had cancelled it out. But in retaliation he had cut away the very foundations of her being, destroyed her completely, and he had not repented at all. Therefore he himself must be destroyed, he and all his works. That was justice, and from the moment when she had first seen the rightness of this final judgement, she had never wavered in her resolution.

She finished typing the letter to Richard Grieve, signed it "per pro G. E. Goff," put it in an envelope, and propped it against the pile of unopened mail, and then went to the kitchen and picked up a box of matches and the tumbler containing the drink that she had prepared for Hector, and walked slowly upstairs.

CHAPTER 16

"I wish you'd never gone there," said Richard.

"So do I." Paula was curled up in one of his big armchairs. "I've done no good at all, and I've made myself so miserable I don't know how I'm going to get through this party at college this evening."

"Must you go?"

"Yes."

Richard filled up her teacup. "If it's any comfort to you at all, which I fear in your present condition it isn't, you have certainly convinced me that Mary isn't sitting there miserably fearing that she's going to lose James because I am going to have the Goff Papers. That's what I was worried about and you've made me feel better about that, for which I am most deeply grateful."

"She didn't seem to me to care what happened to either James or the papers," said Paula wearily. "It was weird. I couldn't make it out at all. And I had this beastly feeling that she was laughing at me. Until we went upstairs to the study. I don't think she was laughing then. And I might have found out what she was really thinking if I hadn't got so worked up and made a fool of myself."

"I wonder why the room affected you in that way," said Richard.

"Don't you dislike it yourself?" Richard did not immediately reply. "You are as good a writer, in your own way, as he is," went on Paula, "but you haven't created a horrible cold desert to work in. You've made yourself a scholar's room, but it's got warmth and feeling in it as well."

"I have sometimes wondered," said Richard, looking away.

"You're all right," said Paula almost fiercely. "You're a bit of a fuss-pot, but there isn't the slightest resemblance between you and an inhuman monster like G. E. Goff."

"Inhuman monster," repeated Richard slowly. "Yes, I suppose he is."

"You've talked to him a number of times. Haven't you ever felt it?"

"Not really," replied Richard, "but then I've only been there to interview him, which is very demanding work and doesn't leave any energy over for picking up disagreeable vibes. But I have to admit that I don't want to stay in that room to work on the papers. When the time comes, I should like to get them all away as soon as possible and put them into the spare room here and sort them out at leisure."

He glanced at Paula as he spoke, and she knew that he expected her to react with interest, perhaps even to suggest that she might come and look through the Goff Papers too in case there was something of interest for her own work.

But she could not show any enthusiasm. At that moment she felt that she never wanted to hear or see anything of the Goff Papers again, and the most she could do was to keep this thought to herself. And yet I have had only a brief glimpse of what it is like to have your life smothered by G. E. Goff, she said to herself; what must Mary feel? And then she remembered her own advice to Mary: Don't marry James, or you will never be rid of G. E. Goff and all his works. Ought she not to be giving the same sort of advice to herself?

Richard was looking a little puzzled, perhaps even a

trifle hurt, by her lack of response, but she could not pretend. If they were to have a future together, it must be founded on openness and honesty. She must say what she thought, but in no way must she denigrate his own life and work.

"You're going to have to take out a mighty insurance policy," she said with a smile, "if you're going to store all that stuff in this flat." And then, more seriously: "I think I shall feel differently about the documents when they are here in their proper home with you. At the moment I feel as if they've got blood on them. Like a sacrificial altar. Do you know what I mean?"

In great suspense she waited for his reply, and was flooded with relief when he said slowly, "Yes. I think I do."

At a quarter to six James Goff, after a very busy afternoon, remembered that he had meant to telephone Mary again before the party started. He lifted the receiver and dialled the number and let it ring for a little while, but there was no reply. This did not worry him, however, because when he had spoken to her a couple of hours previously she had said that she had moved the upstairs telephone extension because the nurse didn't want to be disturbed, and that if he was to ring between five and six, he might well not get a reply. The neighbours across the road had called to ask how James's grandfather was and had invited Mary in for a drink and a change of scene, and she thought she might as well go.

James had been pleased to hear this. It must mean that she had quite recovered from the crisis of last night and was doing what he had often urged her to do, be a bit more sociable and less of a recluse. By the time he got back to Chestnut Close tonight, she might be well enough for him to proceed with his little scheme, which had been so much overshadowed by Mary's shock and unhappiness.

It all seemed rather silly now, that bright idea of his, and the delay would not have helped, but nevertheless he could ask her whether she had noticed anything different in the study and see what reaction he got.

James Goff went off to the party in quite a cheerful state of mind, relieved about Mary, and full of future plans for getting possession of his grandfather's papers if his present little effort should come to nothing. He even felt a little more forgiving towards Paula, and instead of deliberately avoiding her as he had intended, he actually sought her out. But she was deep in conversation with the new professor, and seemed determined not to notice that James was hovering around, hoping to talk to her. Other friends and colleagues claimed him, demanding to know whether it was true that G. E. Goff was dying at last, and if so, what was going to happen to that treasure-house for literary scholars that he would be leaving behind.

James enjoyed himself dropping hints, letting it be known that he had come to a happy understanding with the stepdaughter who looked after the old man. Even though he still had his own doubts, it was pleasant to feel that everybody else was quite sure that he would get the loot.

A few feet away Paula was talking on the same subject to the new professor. Somebody had told him that Mrs. Glenning was acquainted with the Goff family. Was the old man really dying? And was it true that the old family history had been forgotten, and the grandson acknowledged as heir?

Paula replied that she had no information on either point; perhaps James could help.

The new professor, who had his eye on the Goff Papers, or some of them, for the college library, was rather disappointed. He had not formed a very high opinion either of James Goff's scholarship or of his reliability, and, quite apart from that, he himself liked to go about things in a devious way.

Half a dozen miles away, and an hour before these conversations took place, Mary Morrison removed the pillow that she had been holding over her stepfather's head and looked down on all that remained of G. E. Goff. A shrivelled little bundle of skin and bone. There had been a few convulsive movements, but no struggle. She did not think he had even recovered consciousness before he died.

So that part of her task was done. Now for the splendour.

Loose papers burned quicker than papers stuffed tightly in drawers and filing cabinets. She started with the diaries in the black notebooks, taking them down from the shelf and flinging them around, like deck quoits, on the floor near the desk. Then she tipped out the contents of each box file, one by one. Then came the filing cabinets, with their folders full of correspondence dating from many years back. Loose sheets of paper bearing famous signatures drifted onto the growing funeral pyre.

The contents of the drawers of the desk followed, and last of all she opened the cupboard where the manuscripts of the novels were stored. These were the greatest treasures, even more so than the diaries. G. E. Goff had written every one of his works on thick-lined foolscap pads, writing on two-thirds of each page and leaving the bottom third blank for revisions. His handwriting was large, and he had written only on one side of each page, so that every novel took up two or more of these foolscap writing pads.

Mary took each one out tenderly and hugged it to her for a moment in an ecstasy before tearing off lumps of paper to join the great pile round the desk.

When she came to the final manuscript, that of *Last*

Judgment, she paused for a moment. This had always been her favourite among his books, although in those dim days when she had belonged to the everyday world she had actually criticized it to James. It was a story of deceit, disillusion, and despair. It held no hope or light.

Last Judgement should have special treatment. It should flare up in hope and glory now.

Mary tore the pages into small strips, crumpled them up, and tucked them carefully around the stems of the flowers, some pieces right inside the wooden bowl, some wedged higher up the stems in case the flowers did not burn as well as she hoped, and other pieces of paper she dropped outside the bowl, on the desk.

It took quite a long time, partly because of the nature of the task, and partly because there was now such an avalanche of loose paper and notebooks around the desk that Mary kept slipping on it. But the final effect was rather pretty, as if it had been snowing on the flowers and on the surface of the desk.

At last everything was ready. In the middle of the bowl Mary had stuck a few hollow sticks that she had brought in from the garden shed, their ends dipped in paraffin. She took out one of these, struck a match, and carefully held it to the end. The stick caught fire at once and burned well, but not too quickly for her to hold it at arm's length and bring it near to the white seed pods of the honesty. They blackened, but did not flare. Mary moved the stick slightly until it touched one of the scraps of paper torn from the manuscript of *Last Judgement,* and then, as the flames began to leap, she let go of the stick and hastily moved back to the doorway of the study and switched off the light.

There was not, as she had half expected, an explosion, a fountain of sparks as from a firework, but it was rather like a little burning tree, which lit up now here, now there, as the flames darted about it; a fascinating and mysterious prelude to what was to come.

As she stood watching, sparks began to fall on the papers scattered on the desk, and the smoke from the flowers was like that from a bonfire, burning her eyes and making her choke.

Shutting her eyes and coughing, she stepped farther back until she was standing in the doorway of her bedroom opposite; and then, still gasping, she opened her eyes once more to the flaming glory.

The avalanche on the floor was now well alight, and pieces of burning paper were flying around the room, settling on the curtains, the winged armchair, the upright chairs, and the tables. The desk was already in flames, and the carpet smouldering. Nothing, nobody on earth could stop it now. She had fulfilled her destiny. The entire room was ablaze.

For an eternal moment she feasted her eyes upon the fire, stifling her coughs, and then she backed into her bedroom and felt for the tumbler that she had put on the shelf above the wash-basin, for her eyes were streaming now and she could barely see, and picked it up, and drank down the drink that she had prepared for Hector, and she felt the whisky burn her throat in the moments before she slid, strength and consciousness gradually leaving her, to the floor.

It was the family across the road, whom James believed Mary to be visiting, who first noticed that something unusual was happening at Number 12 Chestnut Close and called the fire brigade. By the time they had the flames sufficiently under control to begin to consider a closer inspection, it had become obvious that there could be no human being left alive in that house, and that the top two floors, at least, were extensively damaged.

Among a little group of Chestnut Close residents who were watching from a safe spot farther along the road stood the living descendant of the great twentieth-century English novelist, tall, white-faced, silent and stunned.

Near to him stood a policeman and two short plump middle-aged women.

"Poor man," murmured one of them to her companion. "Fancy coming back to find this! It gave me a most terrible shock when I arrived, Dr. Corbett, and it's not really anything to do with me. But when it's your very own folks . . ."

"Poor James indeed," said the other woman very gravely. Then she added, "But he, at any rate, can't be held responsible for this. I wish I could feel equally innocent, but I can't help feeling that somehow or other I ought to have been able to prevent it."

"You don't think it's an accident, then?" said Mrs. Lowder.

"This was no accident," replied the doctor. "There was an invalid in that house who should not have been left alone in any case. And if he *had* been left alone . . ."

She paused a moment, then said, "You say that Miss Morrison telephoned you and told you not to come till eight o'clock?"

"That's right," agreed the nurse in her quick, rather nervous manner, "and I was very relieved because I had been quite worried about getting away in time, and with Miss Morrison being in charge here, I naturally didn't think that there could be anything . . ."

She, too, let her voice fade away.

"Hector Greenaway," said Dr. Corbett. "He's the person who'll be able to tell us most about it. That is, assuming we don't find Miss Morrison. Or assuming we don't find her alive. Hector Greenaway. He tried to tell me something this morning. He tried to warn me. And I wouldn't

en away the worst of her headache. The tele-
s in the living-room. She collapsed onto the set-
ialled a number.

d—oh, Richard!" was all she managed to say
heard the voice at the other end.

ve just heard it too," he said. And then, as she did
nd, he added anxiously, "Paula—are you all

t migraine."

come and see you? Or would that be too tiring?"
e it," said Paula. "I'm all right as long as I'm not
stand up. But the place is in a terrible mess."
we all," he said. "What can I bring you? Is there
that would ease it?"

as about to say, "Not really," except the tablets
ad already taken, when it occurred to her that it
nfort him a little in the loss of his dearest ambi-
could feel he was being of use to her, so she said
at lemon juice, unsweetened, sometimes helped
ausea, and perhaps he wouldn't mind going into
ostead Stores on his way up the hill.

arrived an hour later laden with flowers and
n assortment of exotic things to eat and drink, in
o the lemon juice. Paula, stretched out on the
h a rug over her, looked at the offerings and
in delight.

ood is for later," he said, "when you're feeling
o you want to talk about it now, or would you
tarted in right away with cleaning up the flat?"
alk," she replied. "Unless you can't bear to see
le."

see anything," he said with deep unhappiness,
Mary Morrison's face, surrounded by a sort of
que hell-fire."

seeing it too," said Paula, and she shifted to one

listen. Oh God," muttered the doctor, passing a hand
across her eyes, "pray God they don't find—pray God he's
alive and well."

"Dr. Corbett," whispered the nurse, "that policeman is
looking at you rather oddly."

"I know, I know," said the doctor, recovering herself.
"There'll be endless inquiries over this, and naturally I
shall tell them all I know. It's just this terrible waiting. If
only they could get in. If only we could know who was
there."

But it was still a long time before the officer in charge of
the operation informed her that two bodies had been
found, but that identification—and here he glanced at the
white, dazed face of James Goff—would be rather an un-
pleasant business.

"Then Mr. Goff must be spared it," said Dr. Joan Corbett firmly. "He's in a state of shock, and as soon as we can
get away I propose to attend to him myself. I think you
will find I can tell you enough for your purposes."

And she murmured some reassuring words to James,
took a tight grip on her black medical bag, set her mouth
in a grim, determined line, and plodded alongside the
uniformed figures into what remained of Number 12
Chestnut Close.

CHAPTE

Paula first heard the news at ei
morning.

She awoke early, with migrai
flicted her during stressful days;
some pain-killers, and then retu
relax, switching on the radio fo

After twenty minutes of Moza
switched her mind off, waiting p
of the world should come to an e
But the name "Goff" came thro
consciousness, and she started u
her aching head with both hands
attention.

It was not a very long news ite
tials. The house of the eminent
of Merit, had been severely dar
Two people died. Mr. Goff hims
from a recent heart attack, and
kept house for him. The cause c
but it seemed to have started in
his most famous works had beer
manuscripts and diaries and corr
kept. All of these precious pape
loss to scholars—indeed the loss
culable.

Paula switched off the radio an
exceedingly weak and dizzy, bu

have dri
phone w
tee and
"Richa
when sh
"Yes,
not resp
right?"
"I've
"Shall
"I'd lo
trying t
"So ar
anythin
Paula
that she
might c
tion if b
instead
with the
the Hai
Richa
fruit an
additio
settee
exclaim
"The
better.
rather
"Let'
the mu
"I ca
"excep
Dante-
"I ke

side to make room for him, and they remained quietly for some time consoling each other.

"You wanted those papers so much," murmured Paula at last.

"Soon I'm going to feel disappointed, but at this moment it doesn't seem to matter. Not in comparison with Mary. Why didn't she escape? Could she possibly have been trying to save the old man? Or some of the papers?"

Paula shook her head and gave a little squeak of pain. "I've got to keep still. It's still not gone. No," she went on, "I don't think that's what happened. I'm quite sure she wouldn't risk her life for either G. E. Goff or the papers. Rather the contrary."

There was a silence before Richard said, "Do you mean you think she was responsible for the fire?"

Paula started to nod, remembered her sore head, and checked the movement. "It seems to fit in with the impression I got yesterday," she said, "but we'll have to wait to find out more about it. I know whom we can ask—the nurse. I got her phone number and address so that you could send her the ticket you promised."

Mrs. Lowder answered the call, and Richard held the instrument so that Paula could hear too. From an excited and confused narrative they gathered that there seemed to be some justification for Paula's suspicion; that the fire had definitely started in the study; that Mr. Greenaway had told Dr. Corbett that he was worried about Miss Morrison and afraid that she was becoming mentally unbalanced; and that, by pooling their information, they had discovered that Miss Morrison had deliberately arranged for there to be nobody in the house but herself and her stepfather from five o'clock onwards.

"What about James Goff?" asked Richard when he was at last able to get a word in.

Mr. James Goff was completely shattered. Mrs. Lowder

had scarcely ever seen anybody so shocked. He had spent the night at his grandmother's, Dr. Corbett going there with him to explain the situation to the old lady, and as far as Mrs. Lowder knew, he was still there. The conversation came to an end at last. Richard and Paula had scarcely had time to digest the nurse's information when the telephone rang, and Paula stretched out her hand for it.

"James!" she cried. "Oh James, my dear, I don't know what to say . . . where are you? At your flat? . . . Yes, I'd love to see you, but I've had migraine and don't feel up to coming out just yet. . . . Yes, of course you can come here . . . an apology to me? What on earth do you mean? Come over right now. Richard's here, by the way. You must try to console each other. . . . Apologies to Richard too? All right. I'm handing over the phone to him."

Paula did this, then sank back against the end of the settee, temporarily exhausted.

"I think you had better come straight here, James," said Richard. "Neither of us has the slightest idea what you are talking about, and the suspense is making Paula's headache worse."

When James arrived he was received with great warmth and sympathy by them both. "Shattered" really did seem to be the right adjective in this case. He's lost Mary and he's lost the Goff Papers, Paula said to herself; two heavy blows at once. But nevertheless she had a sneaking feeling that he was going to perk up again, and when he began to explain what was on his mind, she had the impression that for the time being his losses had receded into the background. James had always enjoyed apologizing, always happy in the certain knowledge that he was going to be forgiven.

"I had this perfectly idiotic scheme," he said to Richard, "of trying to make it appear that you or Paula had stolen some of Grandpa's notebooks. You see, I suspected that he was going to tell you he wanted you to have his papers."

"He did," said Richard, and explained what had happened.

"That wasn't a proper will," said James. "You've got to have two witnesses."

"I know," retorted Richard, "but I took it as having some force in law, nevertheless."

For a moment it almost looked as if they were going to quarrel about it.

Paula intervened. "Isn't it a little absurd to be arguing about an inheritance that no longer exists?"

"Yes. Sorry," said Richard.

"Well, as to that," began James. "But let me tell the tale in the right order. Even if Grandpa had intended to leave someone his papers, he wouldn't be pleased if they decided to help themselves before he died. In fact, he'd be so furious that he would very likely change his mind and leave them to someone else. Petty revenge was always one of his chief character traits. So when Mary was cooking the dinner and the nurse was keeping guard in the sickroom, I went into the study and picked up some of the black notebooks and put them in the car. Then I went and had a meal with Mary, and I told her I was going over to my grandmother's, but in fact I drove back to my flat."

"All the way across London?" put in Richard.

"Yes," replied James, looking rather surprised. "I always go eastwards and come over Tower Bridge. I've worked out a way of keeping off the worst of the main routes. Are you interested?"

"No, thanks," said Richard. "I've practically given up driving. I loathe it. It's just that I suddenly felt that I must be getting very old. Sorry about the interruption. Go on."

"Well, I got back to my flat and was going to hide the notebooks there, and then, at a suitable moment, I was going to tell Mary, if she hadn't noticed already, that something had been taken from the study during the time you two were in the house. And go on from there. But while I was wondering where to put them at my place, I had a far better idea. I'd still got Paula's keys."

Paula gave a little cry.

"Because I'd forgotten—yes, Paula, I quite honestly had forgotten—to put them on the table as you'd asked me to before I left here the other night. So I phoned here, got no reply, decided that you two were probably making a night of it somewhere, and came straight over, with the notebooks in my briefcase. If anybody had been here, I'd have made some other excuse for coming, and just taken the notebooks away again. But there was nobody here."

"That explains why I never found the keys till the evening," said Paula. "What a relief. I'm not as scatty as I feared."

"Are you telling us," said Richard, "that those notebooks are in this room?"

"Yes," replied James, looking like a guilty schoolboy. "I'm terribly sorry, Paula. It wouldn't have worked if you'd been an obsessionally tidy sort of person, but with you being as you are, the temptation to plant them was very great."

Richard looked far from pleased, but Paula burst out laughing.

"Oh James, darling James!" she cried. "You are incorrigible. Don't get uptight, Richard, it doesn't worry me in the least, and it's only thanks to James's daft scheme that there are any of the Goff Papers preserved at all. Where are they?" she went on, looking round the room. "And just how did you propose that they were to be discovered, James?"

"I hadn't thought as far as that," he admitted. "I was

sort of going along one step at a time. They're over in that corner by the dictionaries."

Three pairs of eyes turned towards the darkest corner of the room, under the sloping attic ceiling. The books there had overflowed from the shelves, and were lying in piles on the floor.

"It looks just the same to me," said Paula.

"I tucked them down behind the *Shorter Oxford English Dictionary,*" said James, standing up. "I'll get them."

"No," said Richard abruptly as he too rose from his chair. "I'll get them."

"Sit down. Both of you," said Paula.

Her laughter had quite gone and she spoke without raising her voice, but after glancing at her in some surprise, they both obeyed. Paula continued in a quiet but authoritative manner, as if she were giving a lecture.

"G. E. Goff is believed to have kept a diary, sporadically, over a period of several years during the nineteen sixties, which was the second of the two great creative periods of his life. It coincides with the first years of his second marriage, and perhaps there is some connection between the two. What did he write in these diaries? Notes on the books he was planning? Thoughts about life and literature in general? Comments on the great issues of the day? Or records of trivial little daily events?"

She paused briefly, but neither of the rival scholars dared to interrupt. There was at that moment something formidable about the slight figure in the blue quilted housecoat, pale-faced and dark-eyed from the effects of the migraine, and with the bright hair matted and dull. It was as if she had distanced herself from them since James had announced that all that remained of the Goff Papers was here in this room. It was as if her former feelings for James, and her present and much deeper feelings for Richard, had all been put aside, and she was weighing

them both in the balance, judging them, and also judging
G. E. Goff and everything connected with him.

Judging, not only as a scholar herself, but as a human
being.

"It's the great thoughts about life and literature that are
supposed to be so valuable," she said, "but it's the trivial
little bits that people enjoy most and that get remembered. How many notebooks did you take away, James?"

"Five," he replied, like a child answering a question in
class. "They were in piles of five and I took the first pile,
and then filled up the space by taking some from the other
piles, so that it wouldn't be instantly obvious that something was missing."

"And did you look inside any of the notebooks that you
brought away?" asked Paula.

Under her steady gaze he coloured and fidgeted and at
last he said, "I didn't really have much time, but when I
was in my flat, before I came here, I did just glance at
some of them. Well, why not," he added as nobody spoke.
"He was my own grandfather. And in any case, the diaries
were going to be edited and published. It wasn't like
reading somebody's private correspondence. All right, so
I shouldn't have taken them in the first place, but once I'd
got them—well, I'm quite sure anybody else would have
done the same. You would have. Wouldn't you?"

He turned suddenly on Richard, who replied at once,
"Yes, I'd certainly have started reading them if I'd been in
your position."

"And so would you, Paula," said James, turning back to
her. "You wouldn't have stolen them, but you'd have been
damned glad to have them, and so would Richard. I positively refuse to be looked on as the villain of this piece. It's
not my fault that Grandpa's dead. And as for Mary—"

He broke off, made a grimace, shook his head violently,
and turned away.

Paula's expression softened. "I'm sorry, James," she said. "I'm very deeply sorry."

"You've lost nothing but those bloody papers," he muttered, still not looking at her, "and you've got each other."

There was a silence. Richard looked at Paula, but she avoided his eyes. She had indeed been weighing the two of them up, not as individual human beings but as hunters in pursuit. At the moment when James had pointed out the remnants of the Goff Papers, Paula had sensed in them both the sudden quickening excitement of the chase, and in her revulsion had determined to pull them back into the world of human pain and grief.

But there was no need. James had done it for her, and she had no right to judge him or to try to brush it aside by telling herself that he would soon get over it.

It was Richard who was the first to speak. "I'm not making any claim to those notebooks," he said to James. "As far as I'm concerned, they're all yours."

Paula, who had been sitting tensely upright on the edge of the settee, smiled faintly and sank back with a little sigh of relief.

It seemed at first as if James had not heard, but at last he said, in a low voice and still not looking at either of them, "Thanks."

Then he turned round and looked from one to the other in a bewildered manner and said, "I don't even know that I want them now. D'you know what I mean?"

"Yes, I know," said Richard.

Paula got up carefully from her place on the settee and found that, although she was still weak, the giddiness had quite gone. "I've got a suggestion," she said. "Wait a minute."

She walked slowly towards the corner that James had pointed out, bent down and picked up the little pile of black notebooks from the spot he had indicated, and returned even more slowly to her place on the settee, leaning back and shutting her eyes for a moment to recover from the effort.

"We're all of us to blame," she said at last. "We're all partly responsible for what happened. The question is now, what to do with these diaries? We are the only people who know that they still exist. Everybody else thinks they are burnt."

"James ought to have them," said Richard.

"No, I think Richard ought to," said James.

"I don't feel quite equal to exercising a judgement of Solomon," said Paula, "but I have got two alternative suggestions. The first is that we burn them, as Mary would have wanted. She did start the fire, didn't she, James?"

"Yes. They seem to be quite sure of that. But all the same—the thought of destroying those notebooks . . ."

"What's the second suggestion?" asked Richard.

"That I keep them myself and decide what to do with them after I've read them. Don't look at each other in that superior way, you two. There are such things as women scholars, you know, and I do happen to possess a doctorate in English literature."

"You'll have to do a hell of a lot of research," said James. "You're not going to be able to write a biography just from the contents of those diaries."

"Who said I wanted to write a biography? Who said I was interested in G. E. Goff at all?" She glanced from one puzzled face to the other before going on. "The lives that I want to try to recreate are those of Mary Morrison and her mother. I don't expect to find very much in here"—and she tapped the notebooks that lay on her lap—"but there must be a few entries that I can use. Surely he noted when he married his housekeeper. And there'll be other sources—schools, doctors. I think I'll find something."

She stood up and beamed at them both.

"But I'm not trying to hog these diaries," she went on, placing the black notebooks on the settee. "They'll always be here for both of you to use if you want to, provided you don't take them away. And now I'm going to have a bath. I feel much better and I think I might even be able to eat some of those goodies that Richard brought."

She smiled at them again and left the room.

"I think my grandmother might be able to help her," said James, after a moment's thought. "I'll take Paula along to see her."

"And I've got some material I'd been collecting, tapes of interviews and various other items," said Richard. "She'll probably find those useful too."

And they got up and moved into the kitchen and began to prepare a meal together, and to plan Paula's researches for her, in great harmony and goodwill, as if they had been the closest of friends for all their lives.

ANNA CLARKE was born in Cape Town and educated in Montreal and at Oxford. She holds degrees in both economics and English literature and has had a wide variety of jobs, mostly in publishing and university administration. She is the author of seventeen previous suspense novels, including *Soon She Must Die*, *We the Bereaved*, *Desire to Kill*, and *Game Set and Danger*.